AMONG THE MOHEGANS

AMONG THE MOHEGANS

A Puritan's Tale of Passage

Howard Root

iUniverse, Inc.
Bloomington

Among The Mohegans
A Puritan's Tale of Passage

Copyright © 2013 Howard Root

All rights reserved. No part of this book may be used or reproduced by any means, graphic, electronic, or mechanical, including photocopying, recording, taping or by any information storage retrieval system without the written permission of the publisher except in the case of brief quotations embodied in critical articles and reviews.

Certain characters in this work are historical figures, and certain events portrayed did take place. However, this is a work of fiction. All of the other characters, names, and events as well as all places, incidents, organizations, and dialogue in this novel are either the products of the author's imagination or are used fictitiously.

iUniverse books may be ordered through booksellers or by contacting:

iUniverse
1663 Liberty Drive
Bloomington, IN 47403
www.iuniverse.com
1-800-Authors (1-800-288-4677)

Because of the dynamic nature of the Internet, any Web addresses or links contained in this book may have changed since publication and may no longer be valid. The views expressed in this work are solely those of the author and do not necessarily reflect the views of the publisher, and the publisher hereby disclaims any responsibility for them.

Any people depicted in stock imagery provided by Thinkstock are models, and such images are being used for illustrative purposes only.
Certain stock imagery © Thinkstock

Author Photograph © 2012 Olan Mills, Inc.

ISBN: 978-1-4759-8368-5 (sc)
ISBN: 978-1-4759-8370-8 (hc)
ISBN: 978-1-4759-8369-2 (e)

Library of Congress Control Number: 2013908156

Printed in the United States of America

iUniverse rev. date: 5/7/2013

For my grandsons: Tyler, Graham, and Caleb Root—
at the beginnings of their own life passages

Contents

THE ENCOUNTERS
PART I

Chapter 1

He maketh me to lie down in
green pastures: he leadeth me
beside the still waters.
Psalm 23:2

Badby Village, Daventry, Northamptonshire, England
—March 1630

The workday came early for me, as it did with every dawn. As the early spring sun peeked over the small, rounded hills and dense forests of Badby Village in Daventry, I moved—after a quick breakfast of raw milk and biscuits—off to our family's farmyard to feed the small herd of two cows, a handful of skinny chickens, a few sheep, and one poor horse that pulled our plows and our wagons. As for me, I stood taller than average and, with a build like a rooted tree trunk, easily carried myself to these tasks. My duties, responsibilities, and future were clear—my Puritan heritage honor-bound me to serve my father, Thomas Smythe, and my elder brother, Jacob, both on the family farm and on the weaving loom.

My family called me Jonathan, and as the younger son of this tenant family, I foresaw my fate sealed into a life of servitude to my elder brother. On the death of our father, Jacob—at twenty-five the elder son—would inherit our thatched two-room cottage, the farm acreage, and the weaving, with me left to work for him. I would be left with nothing. I would own nothing—not that there existed a great amount to own. For a headstrong twenty-year-old, this eventual servitude did not sit well with me. My father and brother knew well my feelings, dreams, and plans of colonization and independence in the New World.

Our king, Charles I, had started war with Spain in 1625, leaving our country in massive debt and opening up the possibility of colonization in the New World for adventurous Englishmen such as me. This king proclaimed reforms that resulted in prosecutions and persecutions for all Puritans who did not adhere to sacramental Anglican Church laws. To make matters worse, the lord of our parish, Lord Kingley, caused considerable unrest by his attempts to turn much of the croplands to pasture and to restrict our hunting rights in Badby Wood.

Grumbling to myself over my lot, I much anticipated a secret hunting trip after His Lordship's deer into the surrounding Badby Wood with my good friend Aaron Carpenter; we had been friends since we were weaned. Our small family plots of land adjoined each other and the common tenant area of Badby Village. At least my father and brother, I thought, could not deny me the opportunity to put much-needed meat on the table. To hell with Lord Kingley and his band of ruffians! Poaching deer was only a minor crime, punishable by time in the stocks if caught. Our plan was to not get caught!

A low whistle caught my attention as Aaron bounded into the farmyard. Aaron, slightly shorter than I, was well muscled and had the familiar curly red hair of the village. I noticed that Aaron carried his father's musket with him. A full moon ago, Aaron and I had ventured into Badby Wood on a scouting mission to choose good game-hunting sites. We'd been brutally chased off by Kingley's hired men. Aaron had suffered badly bruised ribs from one of the cudgel wielders.

"A good day to you, Jonathan," Aaron bubbled. Always cheerful, he could put a smile on my face in my gloomiest moods.

"Aye, but keep the noise down, lad. If we stir the elders, we'll never leave the village."

"Come, boy, the early start to this day means His Lordship's boys may be sleepin', so we can sneak past 'em!"

It was a good thought, and Aaron helped me finish off the chores. My father and brother had warned me not to touch the musket and shot, but the sense of adventure overcame my timidity. I sneaked into our thatched cottage, crept carefully across the main room to the smoldering fireplace, and gently lifted the musket, powder, and shot bags from the mantel rack on the fireplace. My father and mother were snoring peacefully in their separate alcove off the main room. Brother Jacob was still snoring on his pallet in the loft above them. My two younger sisters were not stirring in their blissful sleep. I eased myself back across the central room, soundlessly closed the heavy oaken main door, and ventured into the farmyard, where Aaron awaited.

"Off we go with us, and may the Almighty keep our powder dry and our shots straight," I whispered to Aaron with a smile.

* * *

We trotted down the well-beaten main road of the village to the edge of Badby Wood and then quickly disappeared into the cover of the dense forest. Badby Wood had originally been set aside for deer hunting, but of late, Lord Kingley had further limited access to the good hunting areas. Hired bands of Kingley's thugs now guarded and roamed the woods, searching for poachers, further enraging the villagers. Aaron and I knew from our experiences that these thugs were ever vigilant, but we had a plan.

We knew these woods like the backs of our hands. The warm sun had leafed out the massive oaks, increasing the silence in the almost cathedral-like forest. We planned to keep away from the main trails through the forest. The dense underbrush and thickets slowed our progress, but we knew that patrols kept their keen eyes on the main trails. We pushed onward toward our hunting site. The sun had slipped over the nearest hilltop, burning off the morning mists. The calls of familiar birds were the only sounds. As we crested a slight rise, we caught sight of what we had come for—a doe placidly browsing in the clearing directly in front of us. She had not caught our scent or noticed our arrival and continued feeding. I quickly and efficiently loaded my musket and prepared to fire. Aaron, who was following me, had sighted in on the doe before me and had already aimed his loaded musket. Our two shots rang out almost simultaneously. The doe leaped, staggered, and fell. The two shots had thudded into the doe below the shoulder, instantly killing it. We hurried to the animal and began field dressing it.

Intent on our tasks, we were heedless to the men noiselessly arriving. The musket shots ringing out in the forest had revealed our location to one of His Lordship's patrols. A snapping twig alerted me to the approaching danger. I sprang to my feet, the bloodied knife from dressing the deer in my hand. Four gnarled and muscular men approached us on the run. Aaron grabbed for his musket, but two of the men quickly overpowered and bound him. The other two wrestled me to the ground, punching and kicking me into submission. The leader of the thugs—a scarred Irish ruffian named O'Malley, whom we knew to be quick to anger and merciless, based on a previous encounter—displayed a special dislike for English Puritans.

"Out for a little hunting, be you? His Lordship don't take kindly to poachers!" O'Malley snarled, spitting in my face and then slamming his cudgel into my stomach for emphasis. I sank to my knees.

"Come on, boys, let's drag these bastards to His Lordship. He'll deal out the punishment." O'Malley chuckled. They roughly dragged us to our feet and commanded us to move out to the nearest trail. Two of the gang lashed the doe to a stout tree limb in preparation for carrying the evidence back to the manor house.

After an hour of forced march, we reached a two-wheeled pony cart that the thugs had squirreled away. The men threw the deer into the back of the cart and quickly jumped in. They roped us like animals to the back of the cart. We started off at a brisk pace. Uneven terrain, a warming sun, and the quick pace of the cart quickly exhausted us both. Staggering behind the cart, Aaron let out a yell as he fell face-first onto the back of the cart and then smashed his head on a small boulder on the trail. The crunch of bone was sickening.

"Stop the cart, you bastards! He's hurt!"

O'Malley looked back, smiling, and whipped the pony into an even quicker pace. For the next couple of furlongs, I could only watch as Aaron was dragged helplessly along behind the cart. Aaron was in mortal danger, but there was no way for me to help. I tried to pray, as I had been taught, to forgive my tormentors, but my anguish quickly turned to blinding anger. If I survived—and I would survive—I told myself that my vengeance would right these wrongs.

* * *

Aaron's face and upper torso were a pulpy red mass by the time the cart slowed and jerked to a stop in front of Lord Kingley's manor house, Fawnswich Hall. The two-story stone-and-brick manor house, built over a century before, was an impressive structure that included a courtyard and several outbuildings. The sun had reached its zenith, warming the stones of the manor. My pain was only beginning as I stood weaving from exhaustion, praying for signs of life from Aaron. The only sound was the buzzing of blood-hungry flies. O'Malley drove the cart into the courtyard and slowly marched to the entryway, knocked quietly on the massive oak door, and waited. A well-dressed footman soon answered the knock.

With a sneer as he smelled the odor of bloody flesh, he asked for a reason behind the intrusion. "What brings these stinking carcasses here?"

O'Malley fawned and scraped in front of the footman. "Aye, we've brought a present for His Lordship—two prisoners we caught poaching on His Lordship's land. One resisted and had to be dealt with; the other's still breathing. And we offer this fresh deer with regards to His Lordship. We await His Lordship's judgment."

The footman scanned the motley gang, the deer carcass, and the two prisoners. "Go around to the back of the manor. I will announce you to His Lordship."

Without further comment, he slammed the door shut. The gang drove the cart around the manor house to the stable and barns behind it, still dragging Aaron and my exhausted self. Then we waited. Flies soon found the deer carcass and Aaron's body in earnest, and just as I was about to lose consciousness, the footman reappeared, followed by Lord Kingley. Dressed in a velvet black suit with a wide white lace collar and topped with a black cavalier hat and feather, His Lordship looked and acted the regal part of one of the king's lords.

After clearing his throat and dabbing at his nose with a lace handkerchief in repeated attempts to cover the stench, he announced in clipped tones as if addressing a large assemblage, "What do we have here?"

O'Malley quickly answered, "Two poachers, Your Lordship. They await thy judgment."

"It seems to me that the one poacher has already received the Lord's just punishment"—he pointed to Aaron's lifeless and bound body—"but the other needs to face his." Turning to face me, Kingley declared, "What do you say in your defense?"

"My friend and I followed the rightful laws of tenancy to hunt Badby Woods, Your Lordship. We did kill the deer, but …" I stammered as Kingley held up his hand to silence me. *Does Kingley believe he has to judge this crime harshly to stem the rising occurrences of poaching?*

"You have said enough to seal thy fate," pronounced Kingley. "The rights of tenancy have been altered and publicly recorded. Take the deer to my kitchen, bury the one knave on common ground in the village, and then lock this one in the pillory in Badby Village for the balance of the day. I will pen a wood sign announcing his crime to be hung around his neck. We have rendered fair justice." With the proclamation delivered,

His Lordship turned and regally left the yard, followed closely by his footman.

Left gaping after Kingley, I screamed, "This was not justice—not justice at all!" I thought to myself, *But vengeance will be mine!*

Lord Kingley heard my cry, turned, and wagged his finger at me. "Tut, tut, make it two days in the pillory for this ruffian, O'Malley!" Then, with a wry smile, Lord Kingley sauntered back into his manor house.

After finding shovels in His Lordship's stable, the gang unloaded the deer carcass, carried it to the kitchen, and then threw Aaron's body roughly into the cart. The footman returned with a hastily scrawled message fixed to a piece of thin wood:

COMMON CRIME OF POACHING,
PILLORY FOR TWO DAYS
SO JUDGED, Lord Kingley.

They hung this board by a cord tightly tied around my neck.

The thugs set off for the village as I stoically plodded along behind the cart. As we crested a low hill and entered the outskirts of the village, we approached the common burying ground. The gang stopped the cart as a small crowd of tenant farmers and women began to form.

A group of angry village elders stepped forward. One demanded of the thugs, "What is this? What could they possibly have done to deserve this treatment? You cannot be dragging our own like cattle behind a cart!" Yells from the crowd grew louder as the spectators closed in around the cart. The mood of the crowd quickly turned ugly, for they knew the gang members were thugs hired by Kingley to enforce his rulings.

"Go fetch Goody Carpenter," commanded one of the elders. "Free the prisoner's bonds."

The gang began backing away from the cart, and I sank to my knees from exhaustion as my bonds were loosened. Anger and revenge swelled within me.

Now free, I struggled to my feet. In desperation, I grabbed one of the old shovels in the cart and, in a full-arcing swing powered by my remaining energy, brought it across O'Malley's neck! The blow cleanly sliced open his neck, nearly decapitating him. Blood spurted from the huge gash as he flopped to the ground. Totally exhausted, I again slumped to the ground.

However horrified the gang members were at the sight of their leader gushing life's blood from his neck, they were able to drag me to the middle of the village and lock my head and arms into the pillory. I was now a captive to my own follies! A sobbing and shrieking Goody Carpenter clutched frantically at her dead son. One of the cudgel-wielding thugs took the opportunity to aim a savage blow to my head. Pain and blackness were the last things I clearly remembered.

As the crowd of villagers began to thicken with angry protestors, the gang members backed quickly away from the middle of the village and took off running the way that they had come.

"After them!" A few of the more agile members of my village crowd chased after the thugs.

* * *

Still somewhat dazed, I awoke to a pair of sturdy legs standing in front of me. They looked familiar even to my groggy head, and as I attempted to crane my head upward to view the person in total, I saw that the legs belonged to Aaron's younger brother, Samuel. He stood there with his legs spread, hands nervously clenching an ax. *Is he here to avenge his brother's death?* If so, I would not have blamed him.

With a mighty grunt, he swung the ax downward. I closed my eyes in anticipation of the blow. I felt the wind from the ax as it narrowly missed my head. He brought the ax head down on the lock to the pillory and smashed it open. He had come to save me, not to seek revenge.

"Samuel, Aaron and I poached a deer in Badby Woods. It was wrong but not this wrong." I choked back tears of relief. "The sentence for the crime of poaching is not wrongful death! His Lordship's thugs captured and beat us and ended up killing Aaron. It was His Lordship who sent us here—Aaron to be buried and me to the pillory—all for killing a deer! This is not justice but cruelty and vengeance!"

I now fully felt the effects of the beatings, the forced march, the shock of Aaron's death, and O'Malley's killing. I sobbed with grief and anguish, overcome by my own guilt. Suddenly I was free from the pillory.

"Jonathan, I could not stand by and watch you suffer so. Aaron would have done as much."

With his help, I staggered off to my family cottage after taking one last look back at the site where Aaron's body had lain. In my mind, I could still hear the sobbing Goody Carpenter.

* * *

"You must leave, Jonathan, and you must leave now!" My father, Thomas, shook with rage. The timbre of his voice left no doubt as to his sincerity. "His Lordship's men will be back searching for you in no time. You have committed acts of will against God's commandments. You have sinned against the Lord, against your Puritan teachings, and against your family. And, importantly, against His Lordship's recent rulings—like them or not! We must now face the wrath of His Lordship for standing up for you. The gang of thugs will report this incident! You must leave for our family's sake, for the village's sake, and for your own!" I had no answer, for I knew well Father's temper. He shook his head in consternation. "Anne, tend to his wounds; then I will make final decisions."

My father was a tall, lean man with the shoulders of a man who had worked hard and long, day and night in the fields. His blue eyes reflected the sternness and tenacity of a Puritan elder; his beard was streaked with gray. There was no humor to his face now.

I sat on a three-legged stool before the fireplace, naked to the waist.

Bruises and red welts across my chest and abdomen were testaments to the cruelty of Kingley's thugs. My mother carefully washed the abrasions and then gently rubbed a medicinal salve containing chamomile, Saint John's wort, peppermint, and ginger onto the still-throbbing welts.

"Mother, please talk to Father. I do not want to leave!"

She gently whispered, "Take heart, my son. Your father has to care for our entire family and most of the village as well. You acted rashly and disobeyed your father's commands, God's teachings, and His Lordship's laws. My prayers go with you, my son." I greatly loved Mother as much as I respected Father. "I will pack some food and clothing to take with you. Nothing I can say will change the sins, my son."

I stood with some effort and put on a clean linen shirt. I grabbed a doublet outer coat with a cape, for I knew not the weather I would face—or where I would face it. I had originally planned to leave for one of the colonies in the New World by ship, but without money or contacts, I was at a loss. I did know that I would greatly miss my home, my family, and now Aaron.

Father and Jacob confronted me.

"Jonathan, my son"—Father grabbed my shoulders—"you have done great wrong to your family and your village. You have killed a man in anger, a mortal sin." There was a tremor in his voice. "Worse yet, the entire village will be blamed!" He shook me as he talked. I had not anticipated the depth of my father's anger.

"I am about to tell you something I am sure you do not know. You have an uncle—my brother, Richard—who lives in the New World on an island called Barbados. I contacted him previously in an effort to give you a chance in the New World you so sought after. I had intended to inform you later of this plan, but your sinful actions have forced my hand. I made arrangements with him to indenture you to him so that you will have passage by ship to this place called Barbados. I have the papers for your indenture and passage." He thrust the documents into my hands.

"Go to him. He will provide you with work and shelter. He has land

and much work there in this colony. If you are captured on your journey, you can claim him as a relative and request to be sent to him. This is where I believe you should go; that is what you must do to survive!"

I was stunned. *Indentured? Barbados? What does my future hold for me? Will I ever see my family again?* These questions and more raced through my head. I knew the answers would come in part from my flight, my escape from Badby. My rash actions had set me on an unchartered course, a course that I could not refuse to undertake.

Jacob looked at me for a moment and then simply grabbed me in a tight, brotherly hug. He now showed more compassion than I had seen from him in a long time. In doing so, he placed a small leather bag in my hand. He whispered, "It is all I have. May God be with you, my brother." I knew by the weight that the small bag contained the few pennies that Jacob possessed.

Speechless, I stepped back and surveyed the assembled family—Father and Mother; Jacob; and my younger sisters, Hope and Abigail, both very young girls—knowing that I might never see them again. I attempted to step forward to them but could not, for I knew that if I met their embraces, I would never leave them.

"Jonathan," said Father, "go quickly now and head south to Portsmouth through Oxford and Winchester. We will tell His Lordship's men that you headed west to Bristol. That should give you the head start that you need." With that said, he turned his back to me and stared sadly into the fireplace.

With these final words, I stooped, slowly picked up the small bundle from Mother, and silently left the family cottage without a look back. Dusk approached. If I could keep just off the cart tracks in the cover of the hedgerows, I could make some progress before full darkness fell.

This was the start of a lonely journey for me, a young man who had never really left the boundaries of the farms and lands of the village, yet I needed to linger a moment. I desperately needed to visit Aaron's grave site before I left.

I could smell the freshly turned earth on his grave in the common ground, making it easy to find. Kneeling before the grave, I placed my hand on the earth as a solitary tear coursed down my cheek. I could not find adequate departing words for my friend. Wracked with guilt and sorrow over the loss of my friend and my family, I had fallen from grace through the depraved sin of murder. I had also sinned against my father and family and now faced eternal Puritan damnation. *Do I feel repentance for my actions? I pray to God that my flight, my escape, will somehow save my family from Kingley's retributions.*

Through the tears, I grabbed a small handful of the soil from Aaron's grave, placed it in the pocket of my doublet, stood, and turned my back forever on my home, my Badby Village.

Chapter 2

I knew the journey from Badby Village to Portsmouth—a journey I never thought I would make—could take eight days or more over rough cart trails and rolling countryside, through forests and the cities of Oxford and Winchester. As the scion of a tenant farmer, I had no needs outside the confines of my own small village. I traveled only occasionally to market if our small farm produced surpluses to sell, aside from the tithes to the manor lord and the parish. Now I had no choice—I had to secretly travel to Portsmouth and then seek passage to the island of Barbados and my uncle's plantation. I had no time to think this matter entirely through but held a strong determination to follow this new path. The servitude to my uncle seemed almost as distasteful to me as the servitude to my brother, Jacob—again, I had no choice now. The death of my friend Aaron still weighed heavily upon me. As long as the weather held steady and without rain, I could make good time. Any heavy rain, usual at this time of year, would force me to seek shelter in barns and hayricks.

I felt I could make the first leg of the journey, to the city of Oxford, in four days' time. Once I found the main road, I made good time, traveling at night and attempting to sleep during the day under the cover of the hedgerows. I encountered few other travelers. As I dozed off on the third morning, I heard the sounds of approaching horses. Hurriedly brushing myself off, I arose from the field side of the hedgerow where I had bedded down. I worried that Kingley's thugs might be closing in on my trail. Peering through the hedgerow, I discovered a young farmer about my own age driving a small cart, taking his meager produce to market and getting an early start of it. I decided to risk the chance and hailed the driver.

"Good morning. Off to market?"

The young farmer slowed his wagon and curtly nodded his affirmation. Highwaymen were a common danger on these roads. Dressed more commonly now and dirtied from travel and sleeping in ditches and under hedgerows, I hoped that this young farmer would see his way clear to help a stranger in need.

"I am off to Portsmouth to travel to the New World, with hopes and prayers you may find room for a solitary traveler."

He looked my shabby self over and nodded. "Aye, I am to Oxford. If you want, ride along in back." My prayers had been answered. I quickly jumped onto the back of the wagon. I rested and collected my thoughts in preparation for the rest of the journey. The gentle roll of the wagon and the warming sun quickly put me to sleep.

Jolted awake as the wagon rolled to a stop, I groggily awoke to the clamor of a common market on the northern outskirts of the city of Oxford. Thanking the young farmer, I jumped down from the wagon to discover a new world.

I stood there amazed at the scene unfolding before me. Never before had I seen such activity or such filth. Merchants were running and shouting everywhere, with most of the clamor over produce and prices. Animal and human dung littered the cobbled streets. Smoke from cooking fires rose from the numerous chimneys, adding to the haze and stink. Even with all these new sights and sounds, my stomach signaled with a growl that it needed some food since I had finished Mother's provisions the previous day. Perhaps I could find bread and cheese merchants willing to part with their wares for a few pennies. As I wound my way through the marketplace, I spied an old woman displaying a few loaves of bread and a wheel of cheese. I approached the woman and asked her prices.

"Halfpenny for a loaf; a pence for a wedge, if thee so please, milord." She wheezed and spit through blackened teeth onto the ground. I checked the pouch of coins I carried and counted out the moneys. It seemed costly, but my stomach was in no mood for barter. Putting the cheese wedge and loaf into the travel bag, I asked the old woman for directions through the city and then on to Winchester.

"Go past Saint Giles and Bocardo Prison. Don't tarry there—damn drunken students. If you be a Baptist, Puritan, or Quaker, more's the trouble. Find Broad Street and then Saint Mary Magdalene, off onto High Street—that'll take thee out of the city. Keep thine own counsel and you should be safest."

Taking the old woman's directions, I started out, quickly discovering that keeping to the center of the streets was to my advantage since night slops were tossed out of upper-story windows onto the streets below. I barely missed being doused on more than one occasion by foul liquids and projectiles thrown out of windows. Most of the jostling crowds seemed to favor the fronts of buildings under the overhanging upper stories for this very reason. I kept moving swiftly along the street; I found Saint Giles and passed the stinking presence of Bocardo Prison. Looking ahead through the tangled streets, I spied the spire of Saint Mary Magdalene.

Just as I thought I was making progress, I became sucked into a crowd of wild-eyed students focused on a solitary figure. I could just make out this figure as a bearded, middle-aged man of medium build, dressed as a Puritan elder in a russet-colored jerkin with wide white cuffs and collar, stockings, boots, and a tall, stiff-brimmed, conical hat. Violently ridiculed and shoved by these students, the man slowly fell to the cobbled pavement. With some effort, I forced my way through the mass of students until I stood at the inner edge of the crowd.

I was positive the man was a Puritan elder. He was bleeding from the mouth from punches thrown at him. One of the students, who looked and acted like the leader of these ruffians, held a wicked-looking sapling that he planned to use as a whip to savage the elder. Just as the student brought up the sapling to attempt this action, I stepped forward and wrenched it from his hand.

"No more! Let this man be!" With that, I swung the sapling, forcing the crowd of students back. Continuing to swing the sapling, I faced the crowd, hoping to dispel them. The crowd of students lurched forward. I quickly stepped toward the student who originally had wielded the sapling and brought it down on his head, opening a gash that started to bleed profusely. The pack of students, seeing the injury to their leader, quickly began to lose interest in their prey and started to fall back.

"Bind his wound, and let this be the end of it." I glared at the students and held tightly to the sapling. Grumbling and cursing, the crowd slowly began to clear the street.

"Heartfelt thanks, my son." The elder rose unsteadily to his feet. I offered my shoulder and guidance, and we gingerly moved out of range of the crowd of students onto a quieter street. "It's good of you to help. The name is Winthrop—John Winthrop. Who might you be, son?" Hesitating to speak due to fear for my own safety, I responded by giving only my family's surname. Elder Winthrop continued to press me for details about my family, faith, and destination.

"I am probing not to be meddlesome but because of a journey my group is about to undertake to the New World. As Puritans, we are seeking a pilgrimage of new beginnings in a new land where we can practice our faith and live in freedom. We are searching for young, stout-hearted men like you who have the faith and strength and are willing to stand for our cause. Our families are prepared to start this journey within a fortnight. Are you a Puritan by any chance, son?"

I was stunned almost to silence. *Here, just presented to me, is a way to travel to the New World with a group of my peers with similar backgrounds, and the journey is to start almost immediately. I have been blessed by the Lord's goodness, and He has opened this new pathway for me.*

Somehow I gathered my wits about me and stammered an affirmation. Elder Winthrop daubed at his bleeding mouth and said, "Son, let me introduce you to some like-minded Puritans."

I gently helped Elder Winthrop down the maze of streets to an ordinary-looking storefront. Entering the shop, I discovered a group of Puritans of all ages and sexes in animated discussions. Most of the conversations were held among the men, with the women and children quietly lining the walls of the store. Elder Winthrop hobbled to the middle of the room, cleared his throat, and raised his hand to silence the crowd. It became obvious to me that this elder commanded respect and wielded more than simply passing authority.

"I have messages from the Massachusetts Bay Company concerning our departure, and a possible new recruit to introduce to you. First, allow me to introduce a young man who's responsible for saving me from a savage beating—Brother Smythe." Now the center of attention, something that I did not relish, I warmed to the welcoming handshakes as I slipped into the group surrounding the elder. Elder Winthrop efficiently dealt with the important matters of emigration: the fleet of ships, departure times, and the endless lists of supplies required. I soon discovered that this group of Puritans was the Oxford contingent for Winthrop's planned journey to the New World and that departure on a flotilla of ships was set for April from the Isle of Wight, outside of Portsmouth.

This is most welcome news just now presented before me. Providence has laid before me the means to start a new life in the New World! For a brief moment, my thoughts returned to Badby Village and my family there. *Perhaps I can backtrack to Badby Village and tell the family of this good fortune and urge them to accompany me on this fortuitous journey. This could be a new start for the entire family, and the prospects are solid and true.*

A calmer brain took hold, and I realized that Father and the family would never accept anything as reckless or foolhardy as emigration to the New World. Only a major calamity would push them to move. The question of my uncle and Barbados still nagged me. *Perhaps Elder Winthrop has knowledge of this distant island and means to travel there.* As soon as the discussions and questions from Winthrop's flock settled down, I approached Winthrop with this question.

"Good sir, perhaps you could tell me about the island of Barbados and means to travel there? I have an uncle there who might provide shelter and work for me."

"Aye, I do. My son Henry just recently returned from Barbados. He was an unlucky and very costly tobacco farmer there. I would not recommend it, but perhaps you could learn more from him." With that, he turned to a young man only a few years older than I who was standing in a group of young male Puritans excitedly talking about the upcoming journey. Winthrop beckoned the young man over.

"This is my son, Henry, recently returned from Barbados, headstrong but of good heart. He can provide the details you seek. Meet Smythe, Henry, a stout-hearted young Puritan like yourself who salvaged me from the mob." With that, he turned and left the two of us to our discussions.

* * *

Henry Winthrop proved to be more like me than I could ever have imagined. He was married yet carefree, with an unassailable joy for life and the unexpected that I found intoxicating.

"Jonathan, this is a land you can barely imagine!" Henry warmed to the task of detailing Barbados. "The climate is hot for the most part, but there are constant breezes they call trade winds that have a cooling effect on the island. Most of the storms that savage this part of the world pass by this island. The soil is as rich as any soil here in England, perhaps even better because of the mild temperatures year-round that are much favorable to the growing of tobacco crops. The plantation owners use dark-skinned slave labor and indentured peoples like you to work the fields, but for the most part, it is a slow-paced lifestyle. Since the island has only recently begun constructing colonies, the buildings are more than a little rough, but new and better buildings are being built weekly. The plantations seem to grow at an astonishing rate! You are indentured to your uncle there?"

"Aye, my uncle is Richard Smythe. Do you know of him?"

"Yes, and he runs one of the best plantations on the island that grows tobacco. A fine operation he has there!"

"That settles it then—I'm off to Barbados!"

Henry armed me with the facts—everything that could have persuaded me to continue this journey. Barbados sounded like the Promised Land!

"How do I find my way to Barbados? I have my indenture and passage papers with me."

"As it happens, I do know of a supply ship, the *Olive Blossom,* leaving from the Isle of Wight for Barbados the same day our flotilla leaves for the New World. I know the captain and, with a few well-placed words, can attempt to find you berth on his vessel. Since you came to the aid of my father, I feel honor-bound to help. You are not afraid to work or to face challenges of the unknowns?"

For a brief moment, I pondered the question, and then I replied, "I offer my whole being and strengths to the challenges and passages for my future." With slaps on the backs and a quick handshake, we agreed to meet to set further plans.

Elder Winthrop provided me with housing at the inn he resided at, along with meals, so grateful was he for my intercession with the mob of students. I tossed and turned on a bed mat placed in front of the warming fireplace. My mind raced, yet I eventually found the will to order my thoughts, with much-needed sleep following.

The few remaining days passed quickly for me. We all traveled via cart and wagon to Portsmouth in anticipation of the great voyage. Luckily, I carried little of a personal nature with me, for I was kept occupied in helping others in Winthrop's group prepare for their journeys of a lifetime.

When we arrived, the city of Portsmouth and the adjacent Isle of Wight were abuzz with activity: I saw seamen; carters; warehouses; barrels, bags, and sacks of all sizes and shapes; cattle and fowl of all descriptions; and, of course, a virtual forest of masts from ships and vessels of all types and sizes. The tang of the salty sea air was new to me, but I found it bracing. The Winthrop Puritans, over seven hundred souls all told, were to embark on a flotilla of eleven ships with the *Arabella* as flagship, carrying with them the charter for the Massachusetts Bay Colony.

Henry Winthrop, true to his word, helped find me passage on the *Olive Blossom*, a supply ship headed for Africa and then Barbados.

"Jonathan, the *Olive Blossom* is a good ship with a good, decent captain. As indentured, your passage is paid by your uncle and will ensure safe passage and sanctuary. You will need to work some on the ship, but I can see you do not shirk from hard work. Good luck to you! Perhaps we will meet again in Massachusetts!" With these final words, we parted company, both of us off to different points of the compass.

The first week of April 1630 had been selected for departure, the actual day dependent upon the tides and winds. All preparations had been made, all documents signed, stowage arranged, and berths assigned. I found myself wishing I had made the decision to depart with these newfound friends for the voyage to the New World, but I resigned myself to the path my father had chosen for me—the only good choice left for me—and I thought no more of it.

Finally, the day arrived when the captain of the flagship, *Arabella*, made the decision to depart, and the eleven ships slowly followed one another out of Portsmouth Harbor and into the Atlantic. It was a bright day and full of promise. The *Olive Blossom* followed the last ship of the westbound flotilla out of the harbor and headed south. I stood on the deck, watching the last dark line of England disappear slowly from view.

It would be the last view of my homeland. As I shoved my hands into the pockets of my doublet, my fingers touched a small glass vial I had found that I now kept in one of my pockets for safekeeping. It safely contained some of the soil from Aaron's grave.

"Off we go with us, and may the Almighty keep my powder dry and my shots straight," I whispered.

THE CROSSING

PART II

Chapter 3

They that go down to the sea in ships,
that do business in great waters;
These see the works of the Lord,
And his wonders in the deep.
Psalm 107:23–24

Atlantic Ocean—May 1630

The captain of the *Olive Blossom* followed the time-honored route to the West Indies: south along the coasts of France and Portugal, southwest to the Canary Islands, and then, after resupplying at the Cape Verde Islands, westward to Barbados, pushed by the trade winds. A crossing could be made in thirty-five to forty-five days with good winds and weather.

For me, the trip was extraordinary. Travel on the open ocean in a small wooden vessel was fraught with dangers, weather not the least of them, but this voyage had so far enjoyed fair weather—sunny blue skies and blue ocean waters. The blue seas and fair skies did nothing to ease the assault on my stomach. Unused to the rise and fall of the waves and the ship's seemingly random motion, I became violently ill—my stomach contents feeding the fish. After several days of agony, I gained my sea legs, much to the delight of my fellow sailors.

I was assigned seaman's duties aboard the ship, which included a goodly amount of lugging and tugging, scrubbing and washing. We awoke at dawn and began the day's work by scrubbing or swabbing the decks, using cold seawater and stones. The work was grueling but nothing more physically demanding than the tenant farmwork I was used to. I did learn that the ship leaked—and leaked so much that one of the jobs assigned to me was pumping the bilges. Deep inside the ship could be found the bilges and the bellows-like bilge pumps that required constant manpower to rid the ship of cold, stinking seawater.

As I labored through the days, the work took on a rhythm: a day's work, most times out in the open sea air; a ration of something to eat, most times gruel or moldy biscuits; and a place to lay down my head at night, even if it was in a hammock below decks with the sweating and stinking crew. It fit my thinking at the time, and as long as I kept to myself and completed my share of the work, I felt that I would be left alone.

I noticed that the sailors, when given time to themselves, often devoted this leisure time to carving and whittling pieces of ivory. Plucking up my courage, I approached one of the friendlier sailors, called Jim, and asked about the pastime.

"Aye, lad, when the first mate gives us the rest we so need, we pass the time keeping our hands busy—you know, idle hands are the devil's workshop. Some of us use this time working on pieces of wood or ivory we pick up from Natives at some of the ports of call during our passage. At the next port we sail into, let's see what we can find for you to work on."

As I was coiling hawsers on the deck on a sunny afternoon a fortnight into the crossing, the seaman posted as a lookout on the mainmast yelled, "Land off the starboard bow, Cap'n!" I peered off to the horizon and could barely make out the thin strip of black just beginning to appear on the horizon. "It's Tenerife," yelled the lookout. How the lookout knew from that distance that it was Tenerife was a mystery to me. However, the mystery was just beginning.

One of the seamen on deck responded, "*Isla del Inferno*—the island of hell! Look!" I scanned the horizon to where the seaman was pointing and could just make out the tip of a snow-crowned mountain peak rising out of the ocean. The seaman mumbled something and crossed himself, turning away and saying nothing more. Later I was told that the mountain we saw spouted smoke, fire, and cinders like the gates to hell. Earthquakes sometimes shook the islands for days.

As the *Olive Blossom* edged closer to the island, I began to make out small buildings and fishing boats of the port city of Santa Cruz. Trees and flora unlike anything I had ever seen soon came into view—I saw palm trees swaying in the hot breezes, and flowering shrubs in colors unknown to me. The port city was nestled at the foot of a string of sharp mountain peaks; welcoming piers jutted out into the bay. The ship slowly edged up to one of the piers and was quickly tied off by a swarm of shiny, half-naked black longshoremen. They quickly loaded water, fruits, and grains onto the ship. The crew joked with these *chicharrera*, good-naturedly yelling back and forth, bartering for goods like tobacco and fruits.

Jim sauntered over and offered to help me find some ivory or wood to barter for.

"Aye, lookee here, a Native with just what you're lookin' for!" He pointed through the clamor to a bright-eyed young Native boy holding up what looked like giant ivory teeth—way too large for me. I thought I could make a piece of ivory into a container to hold tobacco or powders of almost any type. I could carve my initials into it to make it my own.

"Smaller, boyo?" Jim asked. The lad nodded and produced a hand-sized tooth.

"Just right, don't you think?"

"That'll serve my purposes just right!" I gave the lad a couple of pennies for it.

Back on board, the captain anchored away from the pier for the night to keep the sailors on board the ship. With the outgoing tide, the ship departed for the next stop, which one of my shipmates told me was Cape Verde.

*   *   *

A stiff breeze out of the northeast quickly drove the ship westward to Cape Verde, a horseshoe-shaped collection of parched islands, and the port of Ribeira Grande on the island of Santo Antão. Here, the ship restocked over the following several days with casks of water, salted fish, shellfish, and ground limestone for Barbados. Also, I received an introduction to the misery of the slave trade. A member of the crew pointed out one of the other ships in the port, a Portuguese ship overflowing with Africans bound for Portuguese and Spanish colonies in the Caribbean. The constant wailing of these Africans and the smells of death coming from the vessel were overpowering and physically repulsive. The Portuguese crew tossed dead African bodies carelessly overboard on an almost daily basis. There was nothing I could do but watch their misery for now, but I swore that I would do everything in my power to not condone or foster this curse of slavery. When we stowed the last of the provisions and the islands slipped to the east, I turned my eyes—and, thankfully, my thoughts—to the westward journey.

I worked on my ivory tooth when I found the time, and I was able to roughly carve my initials into it and scrape out and smooth the insides. I found a piece of wood and carved it to fit snugly into the top of the tooth, using small whittled pegs to hold it in place, and inserted a small loop of metal into the top of it. I then strung a length of braided leather from a salvaged shoe, long enough to run around my neck, through the loop. I had created my own waterproof container! I was immensely proud of myself for my imagination and creativity. It then dawned on me that I could use this small container to hold the soil from Aaron's grave. The glass vial that held the soil was taking a beating. I smiled to myself as I retrieved my doublet and dumped the contents of the vial into the waiting tooth container. *Aaron is with me still!*

The amazing journey on the open ocean continued to fascinate me. Powerful blue-green seas rose and fell with fierce gales, which were commonplace. Roaring winds, pelting rain, dangerous lightning, and frothing seas tossed our small ship like driftwood. Fish flew like birds across the waves. The sailors told me that Barbados was nicknamed the Land of the Flying Fish. Large black fish rose with the swells, and their cries and clicks could be heard at night through the wooden hull of the ship. The wind never ceased; it blew at a constant rate, plowing the ship through the ocean, steadily decreasing the time of the journey to Barbados.

* * *

The ship was pushed by a strong early morning breeze into the harbor at Saint James Town, which the Natives called Holetown. I expected some sort of fanfare for the arrival of the crucial supply ship, but the sleepy port was barely awake. As the ship edged up to the solitary pier, a lone Carib man sidled down from the village to help tie off the ship. I was just beginning to discover the slow pace of life on this island, which Henry Winthrop had warned me about.

The dry land felt good after the long sea voyage, but I was not prepared for the heat and humidity of this island. Once the morning breeze died down, the hot sun baked the pier and the village. To keep from passing out from the conditions, I craved a moment of shade, but I was pressed into unloading the supply ship. Hours later and soaked to the skin from perspiration, we had completed these tasks and stood looking at the mountain of supplies heaped on the pier. I was permitted to at last ask for the location of my uncle, Richard Smythe. From some of the locals, I discovered that my uncle lived deep in the middle of the island, on a small farming plantation. Getting there would not be easy, but as luck would have it, there was a small supply cart leaving the next day for the plantations in the interior.

The next day, I left for my uncle Richard's plantation aboard one of the pony carts in the caravan of carts; each was filled to the brim with supplies. Bouncing along the rough and overgrown cart trails through the jungle, I was amazed at the density of the different types of plants and trees, along with the colorful flowers and birds. Away from the steady breezes of the ocean, the heat and humidity became oppressive. Mosquitoes and biting flies made the journey even more miserable. I quickly learned that the blacks accompanying me on this soggy journey would speak only when spoken to and, even then, only in the most rudimentary of manners. They kept to themselves and expected me to do the same. Birds and beasts were everywhere, filling the forests with a raucous combination of sounds far different from the solace of the ocean, with only the winds, the slap of the sails, and occasional cries of command.

By early afternoon, our little caravan reached a sizeable clearing filled with young tobacco and cotton plants. I learned later that this field was only one of many. Women worked the fields, and men handled the more arduous tasks of clearing the jungle for additional plantings. I hopped down from the cart, grabbed my belongings, and scanned the clearing, looking for my uncle. I approached a huge, dark-skinned, and muscular Carib man and inquired about the whereabouts of my uncle, Richard Smythe.

"Over there under that palm tree be Master. Don't you go bothering him none!"

Shrugging off the advice, I approached my father's brother I had never before met. I now faced a man who resembled my father, but his build was thicker and more muscular. He was full-bearded and more tanned and weathered. Because of the heat, he wore only a light linen shirt, baggy linen breeches, sturdy boots, and a large, floppy-brimmed straw hat.

"Good day to you, sir. Jonathan Smythe, Uncle."

"Yes, indeed. I see thou hast made the journey unharmed. That is good. You look fit and healthy as well. Your father has indentured you to me for a term of five years, and there is the passage money to work off as well. You can start your work here by helping to unload the carts you arrived on. See Jonah, my overseer you first talked to. There is a goodly amount of work here." With that, my uncle walked off, yelling at Jonah to get the women in the fields working at a steadier pace. Any expectations of a warm welcome were now forgotten. Jonah made certain that I got the message about working.

* * *

Work on the plantation began before sunrise after meager breakfast meals of curried rice. Jonah, the overseer, typically organized the slaves and indentured workers into work parties—the men cleared and chopped through the jungle vegetation with axes and long-bladed swords called machetes; the women handled the planting of tobacco and cotton plants in the cleared areas.

Earnest work began at sunrise. The backbreaking labor progressed through the heat of the day until sundown with only a brief stop for lunch meals. The climate was broken into two seasons: a wet season running from June to November and a dry season from December to May. The wet season was planting time; the dry season was used for the growing and harvesting of crops. The tropic heat and humidity, the biting and stinging insects and beasts, the fevers common here, and the arduous toil took their tolls on the workers. Most new workers, like me, quickly passed out from the heat. Jonah's whip was the only incentive to keep on working.

Once the acreage was cleared and planted, the fields required tending and weeding. At harvest, all hands were required. There were barns, sheds, and Uncle Richard's proposed new stone manor house to build. The work never ended. My nights were spent in small palm-thatched huts with dirt floors—ten men in each hut. The women, of course, were separately housed, although many night visits occurred, with floggings commonplace for those unlucky enough to be caught.

I received no special privileges because of my relation to the master, Richard Smythe. If anything, the relationship was viewed by the other workers as negative. He preferred that I call him Master Richard in the presence of the other workers and slaves; I called him Uncle Richard during our frequent visits. He was ever vigilant as to the progress of our labors and expected me to fill a day with work, and that I did.

On occasion, after the day's work was completed, he would send word for me to seek him out for short discussions on family and homeland. I would cross the planted fields to meet him at his sturdy two-story wooden manor house. It was not lavish and was furnished sparingly but well. We both enjoyed these meetings, and I found him to be open about his plans for his plantation—to introduce the lucrative crop of sugarcane, which would bring in additional moneys—and positive in his questions about my plans as well.

I distinctly remember one talk in particular with Uncle Richard. It was late on a mild tropical evening, just as the setting sun sent warm embers of red light through the palms and into the veranda of Uncle Richard's plantation house. He was just tamping down the tobacco into the long white clay pipe that he favored, when he cleared his throat to commence to speak.

"Jonathan, you are working out well here. Your father cautioned me that you were given over to temper in some of your dealings, but I have seen none of that here. Your work is good, and you pay close attention to detail. You have learned and worked well and hard, and I, for one, truly appreciate that." We talked—or, rather, he talked and I listened—and he laid out the plans for his still-growing and prosperous plantation. "I see no reason why you would not continue here once you have fully completed your indenture. You know what has to be done and how to efficiently get it done. Even Jonah has complimented you to me."

"I appreciate the kind words, Uncle, but I made a pledge to myself on the crossing here that I would not make fortune at another man's expense. The plantation here could not succeed without forced slave labor. True, there are indentured workers here, but their lot is not much above the slaves you own. I see my future in my own hands, through my own work, with no mastery of another involved. Do you understand me?"

"What say you, lad? No slaves? You be foolish to think that! No work would ever get done if you had to hire it out! There'd be no money at it! It's foolish, foolish talk!" He usually smiled and nodded when I talked of my plans; I had never seen him rant on in the manner he did that night. I must have offended his nature. Truth be told, I believed that his reaction had nothing at all to do with slavery or indentured hands but with my intentions to leave to seek my fortunes elsewhere. I learned through our discussions that he had married, but his wife had recently died, leaving him childless and without a male heir.

I found few friends among this lot of humanity. We labored without much talk; no laughter or singing filled the fields. These indentured were a mixed lot—mostly white males, some Irish, some English—and there were the criminals, sentenced to terms of backbreaking labor for their crimes. We were all poor as dirt and none of us glad to be in Barbados. Of course, the indentured all had terms of indenture that had to be worked off, usually in five to seven years, with freedom of sorts at the ends; most remained here and hired themselves out for meager wages to these same masters and plantations. Some work, even this work, was better than no work at all. It was a savage existence for most.

For me, this labor not only hardened my muscles and my hands but also firmed my dreams of freedom on my own lands in the Bay Colony. I spent hours dreaming of fertile lands that I could call my own and on which I could raise a family with no tenancy, no tithing, no slaves, and no master. These lands would be my lands, where I could hunt and fish without penalties. These dreams drove me through the endless days of endless labor—days that I knew would slowly turn into years.

Chapter 4

The first two years on the plantation passed by with the learning and honing of planting and harvesting skills to the point where I became a vital member of Jonah's work parties and vital to my uncle Richard's success. I relished the skill it took to work with the machete day in and out. Work continued on clearing the acreage to the point where only a small number of the men were utilized for those tasks. Drying sheds for the tobacco harvest needed to be built, along with storage barns for the cotton. Master Richard's stone manor house construction would start soon. My thoughts continually turned to my family in Badby Village and the turmoil that my murderous actions might have caused for them. I thought it most likely that Kingley's thugs had returned to terrorize the village and impose harsher restrictions on daily life. To what extent, I had no way of knowing. I prayed that my family would take heart and prepare to leave. I requested of Uncle Richard that he keep me informed of any letters he received relating to our family. He agreed, but little communication from the outside world arrived for either of us.

I thought that finding friendship was out of the question in this land with the type of workers I was forced to work alongside, but I was wrong. At the start of my third year on the island, a new group of indentured workers appeared to help flesh out the workforce, which had been depleted by deaths, diseases, and indenture terminations. One of the new workers was an Irishman. If Aaron Carpenter had had a long-lost twin, this man would have been it. Shorter than I, with Aaron's build and red hair, Shaun M'Gey boasted the same cheerful and rambunctious personality. It seemed that M'Gey had run afoul of an English magistrate in County Cork, Ireland, for "punchin' the stuffin' out of an English tax man," as M'Gey put it; he found himself sentenced to five years of hard labor as a result. He was shipped out to Barbados to serve his sentence. Lucky for me, he ended up at Uncle Richard's plantation. Of course M'Gey got into trouble with Jonah right from the start.

It seemed that Irishmen like Shaun had an inherited dislike for authority, and Jonah was the authority for the workers. The first time I met M'Gey, he was arguing with Jonah over punishment that Jonah had meted out to another worker.

"Yah canna go whipping people just cuz yah feel like it, yah know," exclaimed M'Gey. Although shorter than Jonah, M'Gey was standing right in Jonah's face. Jonah, for his part, was somewhat bemused by this show of bravado from a worker, but his reaction quickly changed to anger when M'Gey did not appear to back down.

"Get back to work, you damned fool, M'Gey," ordered Jonah, "or you'll get a taste of this yourself!" Jonah thrust his whip into M'Gey's face, pushed him back, and uncoiled the whip in preparation for a punishing blow.

I jumped into the fray and pulled M'Gey away. Whipping as a punishment was commonplace, but we desperately needed the extra hands for all of the work on the plantation. We could not lose able-handed workers even for a day.

It took some effort for me to calm M'Gey down. I tried to talk some sense into him by first introducing myself.

"Smythe—Jonathan Smythe—indentured out of England," I said, attempting to sound calm. "Been here for the past two years."

"M'Gey—Shaun M'Gey—enslaved out of Ireland," M'Gey mockingly countered. "A wild geese I be, just landed." The *wild* I understood, but *geese* I did not. Now that humor had gotten control of his temper, I dragged M'Gey off to a pile of cut stones before he could start further trouble. Out of range of Jonah, we were able to quickly tell our stories to each other while stacking the cut stones. And it felt as if our stories were cut of the same cloth. True, we were of different faiths—M'Gey was an Irish Catholic, and I was an English Puritan—but our family histories were similar. We both came from tenant farmer families; both families feared reprisals due to their faiths; and both M'Gey and I had faced the challenges of oppression with violent acts and were now paying for those acts.

"Where did the 'wild geese' come from?" I asked, not knowing what to expect for an answer.

"Irishmen who are forced to travel to other lands are called wild geese," he explained. "We search for freedom. Hopefully, one day, we may return to our homes, yet our homes are always in our hearts, always with us, and we always know the true pathways home. I have yet to find my freedom, but I will not rest until I do, lad." Here again M'Gey and I were similar, except I did not dream of returning home; the search for true freedom was an ongoing quest for me, seemingly to be found farther and farther from home.

* * *

As the weeks turned into months, M'Gey and I found ourselves working more closely together in a variety of tasks; it was all hard work and never ending, but we took heart in our evenings, for we shared the same hut, permitting us to discuss our lives and our dreams. M'Gey came from a huge family of ten children, he being the youngest, born to a life of hardscrabble farming and sheep tending. He faced the same roles as did I, with the bulk of the slim inheritance gifted to the eldest son.

We talked often at night, our only true rest time, when not exhausted from the day's labors. One night, M'Gey ranted on about his background.

"You damned English pressed me into the military as a youngster.

No youngster should be forced to endure the hardships and horrors of the wars that I did in Holland and Germany. I am lucky to still be whole and have me senses about me! But alive I am and glad of it! You know, lad, we Irish have this different view of living and life, heaven and earth. We have a saying: 'Heaven and earth are only a few feet apart, but in thin places 'tis even shorter.' These thin places are special places where real wisdom, tranquil peace, and freedom are revealed. My thin place may be a thick place for you. And, lad, you cannot search for and expect to find your thin place; you won't find it that way—you have to stumble on it. Once you happen on it, you will know it! It will be like a dream come true, lad!"

I fancied that this was more of M'Gey's Irish nature foaming over the top, but the more I thought about it, the more it made sense to me. *The unbending, almighty Puritan God and obedience to His will somehow do not now fit into my search for freedom—this search for my own thin place, my own freedom.* I did not think I would find my place here on Uncle Richard's plantation or anywhere in or near Barbados. *Could my thin place possibly be found in the colonies?* Like M'Gey, I would not rest until I found it or, more likely, it found me.

M'Gey and I continued our talks about our dreams and futures when we could or were allowed to in the days and nights that followed, and we found that our separate future visions were closely shared. These talks not only helped us to pass the time but also provided us with small glimmers of hope for our futures. Without this hope, I would have become like most of our fellow discouraged and downtrodden workers. M'Gey was searching for a place where he could be his own man with his own future, dictated by no other. That was precisely my vision for a future as well, and we both believed that the new English colonies might be fruitful places for that search to continue.

* * *

As luck would have it, in our second year working together, Shaun M'Gey contracted the swamp fever, a fever that I had been fortunate to miss. M'Gey came down with a flushing fever, vomiting, and bodily weaknesses, making him unable to withstand any type of work. For several days, his fever raged. As he became weaker, he became delirious—one night, he called for his mother and friends in Ireland. He grabbed me by my shirt and pulled me close to his face.

"Jonathan, lad, never rest until you find it—the thin place. Promise me you won't give it up!"

I tearfully promised him the best I could. Shaun looked and acted as if he were dying.

The next day, his fever continued to rage. In a panic, I asked Jonah for a cure for this fever before work for the day started.

"We got cure for that"—Jonah eyed me suspiciously—"but don't know if you be liking it!"

"What do you mean by 'liking it'?" Now I was suspicious.

"Pretty nasty stuff the woman uses, but it do cure!"

"Send the woman to our hut as soon as you can," I pleaded. "Poor M'Gey needs the cure!"

When I returned to the hut after the day's work, I found M'Gey sitting up on his sleeping pallet; he was as weak as a baby but better than when I had left him.

"That was some of the ugliest-tasting medicine, given by the ugliest-looking woman I've ever had the luck to endure!"

"M'Gey, I can see now that you are feeling better!" We both laughed. It was good that Shaun was on the mend and back to his old ways.

M'Gey was not without skills and talents besides his bantering and feistiness. He proved to be an excellent stone mason—a skill, he divulged to me, that came from his war experiences in breaching and building defensive positions. This skill soon became apparent, for he was pulled from field duties to manage the building of Uncle Richard's stone manor house. Through his efforts, I was pulled off the field work as well to become a stone worker under his tutelage. Together we worked long and hard on the plans and construction of the house under Uncle Richard's care and guidance.

The house was designed after the popular Spanish architecture, with a stone ground floor, and contained a vestibule; a living room, or great room, with a patio; and a kitchen. Stairs led to the second floor, which was built of local timbers and plastered with stucco on the outside. The second floor overhung the first floor and included a balcony and roof terrace. The large, airy rooms were set off with mahogany floors imported from Spanish South America; bedrooms could be found on the second floor. Clay tiles capped the roof, and louvered shutters completed the windows.

The construction process was a learning experience for me. M'Gey taught me how to fit the stones and mix the mortar. The openings for doors and windows took the most patience, as well as fitting the timbers for the second floor. M'Gey was pleased that we could work together and delighted in his role as tutor.

My uncle was well pleased with the building—so much so that his bragging and the showing of his new home to the neighboring plantation owners caused increased work for M'Gey. M'Gey was soon off to other plantations, constructing homes all over Barbados. I remained behind because the end of my term of indenture was near. I saw M'Gey only fleetingly as he passed through on his way to another construction site. Finally, he was gone and the Irish laughter with him. The last I knew of him, he was still searching for his freedom and his thin place.

THE HOMECOMING

PART III

Chapter 5

But the Lord sent out a great wind
into the sea, and there was a mighty tempest
in the sea, so that the ship was like to be broken.
Jonah 1:4

Smythe Plantation, Barbados—June 1635

Hazy morning sunlight was just beginning to filter through the jungle canopy onto my straw sleeping pallet as I awoke with a smile on my face. This day was to be the beginning of the rest of my new life. By my calculations, I had met the indenture demands of five years from Uncle Richard and had earnestly worked off the cost of the passage.

He had been a hard taskmaster but a fair one, demanding that his workers spend long hours under the broiling tropical sun, clearing jungle undergrowth for the planting and growing of tobacco, cotton, and new sugarcane crops. I had recently seen my image in a small mirror in my uncle's house. The sight had been amazing, for the toil under the tropic sun had caused my hair and beard to lighten and lengthen as my skin tanned and darkened. I knew my muscles had grown and hardened. I believed I looked more like a Carib or a Spaniard and bore little resemblance to the young, stout English lad who had first crossed here.

To my credit, I had mastered the tasks and helped my uncle's plantation grow and prosper. I had helped M'Gey plan and build my uncle Richard's stone manor house, which was now complete. My talks with Shaun M'Gey had cemented my resolve to journey to the new colonies and plantations, where I would begin seeking out my own future on my own lands. I no longer prayed for God's guidance or for His blessing. My future was in my own hands. With a little luck and hard work, I believed I could gain my dreams. I might even stumble upon my thin place there in this New World.

My talks of late with Uncle had focused more and more on my plans for my future—the places I wanted to see, the work I planned to do. Uncle had warmed to me, confiding to me in earnest about his own future for his plantation. I needed to address my final decisions with him.

I walked out of the hut I had called home for the past five years, crossed the plantation to the new manor house, and knocked on the main door. Uncle Richard answered the knock.

"Come, Jonathan, let us talk of your future plans." He ushered me into the great room, where two chairs awaited and a soft breeze blew through the house. "I see, Jonathan, your indenture has run its course. You seek your freedom dues?" Uncle Richard looked at me with a steady gaze.

"Yes, Uncle, that is so. I would like to ship out to the Massachusetts plantation and seek my fortune and future there."

"I had hoped you would consider staying here with me. As you know, I have no heir, and your work here has been most sufficient; the beautiful manor house is just one example. Now, since your indenture is complete, you could continue to work as a full partner here, take full share in the goodly profits with me on the plantation, and, at my passing, inherit sole ownership. The offer is a good one. Surely you have no equal offer in any of the colonies."

"Your offer to remain here is a reasonable one, but I see my future lying elsewhere. My future is in this new land to the north, where I hope to have the freedom to work my land with my own hands as I see fit. I know of a vessel that is planning to depart shortly in a day or two for plantations there. It is my hope to be a part of that journey."

"I have just received a letter from my brother, your father. It should be of considerable interest to you. If you like, I will read it."

Uncle Richard removed the now-crumpled parchment from his pocket, cleared his throat, and proceeded to read the following aloud:

September 14, 1633
Dearest Brother Richard,

I hope this letter finds you well and that my son Jonathan is well. This letter will inform the both of you that my beloved wife and Jonathan's mother, Anne, has passed this part of her journey to the Promised Land, and her burial took place this week past. She will be greatly missed by all her family.

The situation here in Badby Village has worsened with each passing year. His Lordship has enforced stricter tenancy rulings and made life here much harsher. He has taken our arable land for grazing of his own sheep and cattle. Our faith is in our future but not here in England. Our Puritan beliefs have been challenged. Our family and several other families in Badby parish have decided to emigrate to the Massachusetts Bay Plantation in search of a better and freer life, with departure settled for this month's end. It is in our prayers that, with the Lord's guidance, this journey will bear fruit. It is our hope that Jonathan might see fit to join us in this journey to the New World at the end of his indenture to you.

As always, your brother,
Thomas Smythe

"I can see now your full reasons for your departure, Jonathan. I am at a loss to stop you, knowing your family's destination. So be it. Freedom dues should pay for your passage."

*   *   *

The news that my family had journeyed to the Massachusetts Bay Plantation was joyful news to me. If I could seek out passage to this colony, our reunion would be heartwarming and long overdue. My mother's passing tarnished this joy, but the thoughts of reunion with the rest of my family were overwhelming. With a light heart as to my prospects, I made preparations to depart the following day. My last visit to the manor house to bid farewell to Uncle Richard was warmer than anticipated, for he guided me into his parlor with a fatherly arm about my shoulders.

"I wish you well on your decision, Jonathan, to move on to the colonies in the wilderness of the New World there. I tender you your freedom dues to help pay for your passage there." He handed me a small bag of gold coins. "I also have crafted a special gift that perhaps you will treasure as a reminder of your excellent work here and as an offer to one day return here to this plantation to claim your rightful place."

With that, he turned and pulled a package from a satchel he had kept hidden behind him and handed the package to me. The package contained one of the most beautiful machetes I had ever seen. Its curved, razor-sharp metal blade glinted in the sun and was topped by a magnificent, intricately carved bone handle grip. The machete's top-grade, well-stitched cowhide sheath contained a small pocket for the necessary sharpening stone.

"As you know, Jonathan, and as we have discussed, I believe your future lies here, but know that my offer to you still stands. Go with God, Nephew." With his greetings to his brother, my father, and my family, we heartily hugged and parted ways.

My spirits were buoyed by this new passage opening before me, but as with any departure from a place where one has lived and toiled for years, there was a bittersweet taste to it. I would miss mightily my talks with Uncle Richard and my friendship with Shaun M'Gey. The time was now in front of me to face my passages anew.

The journey by pony cart to the port of Saint James Town was as arduous as I remembered; we started out in the cool of the morning but crossed the heart of Barbados during the midst of the day's heat and then rain and finally arrived at dusk. We found only a sole, somewhat decrepit-looking brig mooring at the pier. *Surely this cannot be the ship.*

To my untrained eye, on closer inspection, it looked in disrepair, with poorly patched rigging, but the crewmen seemed busy loading tobacco, cotton, and local fruits on board. As I approached the ship, a closer inspection of the appearance of the crewmen gave me serious misgivings. They were a sad collection of the dirty and undernourished from a wide range of ports. I asked a sickly-looking soul for the captain, and he directed me to a short, stocky Dutchman engaged in a furious discussion with a crewman.

"You'll do as I say, or I'll have yah drawn and quartered, mate! Get these men working, for we leave on the tide. We'll have no more talk of this!"

Not wanting to interrupt, I turned to leave, but the captain spied my approach and hailed me.

"And in God's good name, what do you want?"

I mumbled, "Gain passage to Massachusetts plantation."

"We sail with the tide only to Dutch New Netherland. Find passage from there."

Not wanting to miss my only opportunity, I made a quick bargain for passage, collected my belongings, and boarded the vessel with grave misgivings but a light heart. I spent a sleepless night on board, not wishing to close my eyes to the scurrying of rats. With the early morning tide, the overloaded ship lurched out of port. A stiff breeze and a gorgeous red sunrise soon gave flight to my misgivings.

*　　　*　　　*

As the day progressed, the skies darkened, the gentle breeze changed as if by magic to a shrieking gale, and the water darkened with huge, foaming waves. The rise and fall of the ship with the increasing height of the waves caused the bow to sink more and more into each wave trough. The gale shredded the remaining sails, and with a crack, the mainmast was sheared, taking with it the ship's wheel. Without sails or rudder control, the overloaded ship began to take on water. A huge wave foundered the ship, and without warning, the sad vessel began to sink.

The captain, now without a wheel to steer, commanded the abandonment of the ship. With some difficulty, a rowboat was lowered. The captain and crew piled in—without a single thought for me—and the sailors began to frantically man the oars. The rats had deserted the sinking ship! I was the only human left on board!

The next wave threw me violently into the churning ocean waters. I gasped for air. My hand struck the sheared mast and yardarm. I clambered onto the flotsam and lashed myself with torn rigging to the shattered mast. I watched in sheer terror as the ill-fated vessel sank out of sight with only a slight hiss. All I could see were the wildly tossing waves. There were no cries for help; there was nothing! The captain, the crew, and the rowboat had all disappeared. I was alone and terrified. The rain pelted me like wind-driven pebbles. Somehow I floated in the shrieking gale and on the tossing waves for the rest of the day. With the setting sun, the storm diminished, blowing itself to the west. Exhausted, I fitfully slept.

As the sun rose for the second day, I awoke shivering but still clinging to life. Here I was, alone and lashed to the partial mast of the ship; God knew where I was or for how long I'd been floating! I had silently mouthed every prayer that I knew to my God. The sea was now calmer, and the rising sun warmed my battered and bruised body.

My thirst grew. My tongue swelled, caked to the roof of my mouth, and breathing became more difficult. Water, thirst-quenching water, was all that my thoughts focused on. I knew I could not drink the seawater.

I tried to think the pain away. The sun baked me as it rose higher. *Could it possibly get any hotter?* My thirst grew larger, and my mind wandered to England and scenes from childhood. *There is my brother, my friend Aaron, Father, and Mother—all in the flesh, all too real.* Then the sounds began. I heard music and singing. *And M'Gey is there, singing his heart out. Heavenly hosts? Am I losing my mind? Or is it already lost?*

"Oh my dearest God and Savior, please save a poor wretch from this cruel fate!" I closed my eyes and awaited God's mercy. Then, luckily, I slipped into unconsciousness and saw and heard no more.

* * *

I must be dead. I vaguely saw the faces of the Father, the Son, and the Holy Ghost. They were staring down on me from a bright blue background filled with fluffy white clouds. I feared I was dead and possibly in heaven. I felt water splashed onto my face—*baptism again.* My vision cleared as the water cleansed my salt-encrusted eyes. I could just make out that I lay on the deck of a sailing ship and that the Holy Trinity consisted of three sailors—three ugly sailors at that.

"*Muy loco! Muy suerte!*"

I later learned they were saying, "Very crazy! Very lucky!"

I croaked, "O my God in heaven, I'm alive! I'm saved!"

The little remaining moisture in my body coursed down my face in the form of tears. The three sainted sailors mercifully gave me a small amount of water to drink. I was too weak to sit up, so they helped me to a sitting position.

"Our lookout spied the debris. *El Capitán* steer ship closer. We find body lashed to mast. We think you dead, but Pablo here see you breathing. *Muy suerte!*"

Astonished, I looked around and caught sight of a flag flying stiffly from the mainmast. It was the flag of Spain! At least it was not one of the ships piloted by cruel and bloodthirsty pirates that I had heard terrorized these waters. The three sailors dragged me to a shady spot on the deck, along with a water bladder and bread, and there I stayed, slowly recuperating. My clothes were stiff from salt and rubbed my skin raw—skin that was already sore from the salty water I had endured. Fresh water helped, but that was limited on any sailing vessel, so it would take weeks to heal. The sailors kindly gave me some ointment to rub on my skin, which mightily helped my condition. I was able to scavenge some castoff clothing, which eased my suffering somewhat. I was fortunate that my machete and tiny bag of freedom dues from Uncle had survived the ordeal. Even given these conditions, I felt lucky to be alive.

My mind wandered over thoughts for my future: *Am I a captive, a prisoner of Spain in some ill-conceived war between England and Spain? Why would they keep me alive only to later torture and kill me? I have no important military information to confess. Or is it simply an unwritten law of the open sea to rescue hapless people like myself?* I would need to find some answers.

After several days of food, meager amounts of water, and rest, I was strong enough to move stiffly around. We were sailing leisurely, to be sure, but I was aware, based on my sightings of the nighttime skies, that we were heading in a northerly direction. I sought out the captain, who spoke some English, to learn details on our destinations.

"El Capitán, where are we bound?"

"Amigo, His Majesty King Phillip sends us on a mission of great importance to Hispania, north to the America's coastline to explore and map the English and Dutch colonies there. You are English, no? Do you know of where I speak?"

Again, my luck could not have been better. "*Sí*, El Capitán! It is where I had hoped to journey and seek my fortune—in the Bay Colony there. How fortunate for me that you plucked me from the sea after the sinking of that rat-infested Dutch brig bound for New Netherland. I owe you my life and my future, El Capitán!"

"*Sí*, that is true," replied El Capitán with a smile. "We found that you were not far from death's door, but, luckily for you, you have survived.

In return for your salvation, you could pay us a small amount for your passage, and perhaps you may be able to help us in our mapping, no?"

With a sigh of relief, I readily accepted this offer. From my meager, salvaged freedom dues, I was able to pay El Capitán the small amount he requested. It was only later on, after I had composed myself, that I thought of the strangeness of El Capitán's mapping mission. *Are they mapping the colonies for possible military attack?* I knew that Spain and England were always at odds. *Or perhaps trade routes?* I could comply with the captain's intentions or face being placed in chains—or worse. It was an easy decision to make.

As the weather and waters cooled, I realized that the vessel quickly approached a more northern clime. The mapping process now began in earnest. My job was to take periodic soundings, which required me to stand at the bow of a small rowboat tethered at some distance from the ship and throw out a weighted rope that sank to measured depths. I, in turn, called out these measurements to a designated scribe on the deck. The captain was on board, using a brass spyglass to view and take measurements as we passed along the coastlines.

The weather was warm, the skies fair and a beautiful shade of blue, and the days passed quickly. My final home destination, I hoped, could not have been far off. We passed close by the English colony at Jamestown and the large and sheltered bay there—called Bahía de Santa María by the Spanish, and Chesepiook by the English. We mapped to the south of the busy Dutch colony of New Netherland, my ill-fated original destination, at the mouth of Hudson's River.

To the east of this colony, jagged, forested coastlines with major rivers that pushed into the sea came into view. As we sailed past, I noticed that civilization of a type I was familiar with could not be seen from my vantage point. The huge scale of the lands that I saw from the ocean greatly overwhelmed me. There looked to be room for colonists and hosts of other peoples from Spain, England, France, and Holland to settle and grow here.

As we finally rounded a sandy, hooked peninsula, El Capitán announced that he would anchor the Spanish vessel some distance offshore so as not to alarm the English colonists of the Plymouth colony there. Here again, I could espy no colonists or hints of their settlements.

Luckily, the day broke sunny and warm with a placid sea as El Capitán ordered the lowering of a small rowboat. I bid him the fondest of farewells with many thanks for his generosities, gathered my meager belongings, and clambered down the side of the ship. Several members of the crew rowed me ashore to a narrow spit of shoreline some distance from where they said the English village of Plymouth was located. As the small boat nosed into the rough gravel beach, I happily splashed ashore, feeling for the first time that I had finally reached home. I turned and waved to the departing rowboat quickly disappearing from sight. Now it remained for me to somehow search out my family and start my life anew.

Chapter 6

Massachusetts Bay Colony—July 1635

The countryside through which I traveled was thick with almost impenetrable glens and forests. I saw beasts and birds too numerous to count—and some that defied counting—and there were signs of civilization. A thin wisp of wood smoke just cleared the tops of the trees. Suddenly, a solitary male figure appeared—tall, muscular, and naked to the waist, with long, shining black hair. His dark skin glistened in the sunlight, and he moved with a grace that I had never before seen. Just as suddenly as he had appeared, he disappeared like a wisp of smoke.

I continued trudging along the beach, hoping to again meet with this strange figure. As I rounded a point of beach, a clearing appeared. I saw several figures moving about, and they appeared to be clothed as Englishmen.

"Halloo," I shouted in greeting. I expected a warm greeting but forgot that I was dressed as, and had the appearance of, a Spaniard. One of the men ran for his matchlock musket. Another menacingly grabbed his ax.

"Halt, come no further," commanded the man leveling his musket.

I fell to my knees with arms spread out wide. "Please, I mean you no harm. I search for my family, and that is all!"

"He speaks as one of us but does not look it!"

The men exchanged worried glances. The man with the ax had fear of the unknown in his eyes.

"And, look, he's armed—he carries a short sword!"

"The name is Smythe—Jonathan Smythe. My father is Thomas Smythe, recently of Northamptonshire. Do you know of him?"

The other man lowered his musket and cautiously signaled me to further approach.

"We do not know of this man, but how be it that you come here?"

"I was on passage from Barbados to New Netherland, when the ship foundered and sank. A Spanish ship that was charged with mapping along the coastline plucked me out of the sea and brought me to shore south of here. I have been walking the beach ever since in hopes to find the English plantations and my family."

"A strange tale if I ever heard one. Let's take him to Standish and Holmes to see what they can make of him."

For safety's sake, the men took my machete, bound my hands behind me, and, with a rope around my neck, led me without further ceremony or discussion in search of their two militia commanders, Captain Myles Standish and Lieutenant William Holmes.

* * *

On the journey, our curious-looking group of men passed close by several villages with new cottages in the process of completion. My guards spoke little between them or to the settlers we passed. I noticed that both men and women were hard at work, raising the simple cabins and clearing the land for plantings. Some cattle could be seen. I figured these must have been new families who had just arrived, staking out claims for lands.

Finally, we arrived at a palisade surrounding a rather large village the men called Duxbury. Captain Standish was not to be found, but after some searching, they found Lieutenant Holmes in the process of training his militia.

"Sir, we found this man who calls himself Smythe on the beach south of here. He says he is from Barbados and is looking for his family, but he looks like a Spaniard and was carrying this short sword. We thought it best to bring him to you."

"Aye, untie him and bring him forth."

I approached the man called Holmes, a tall, slender man not much older than I; he had a handsome curling mustache and beard. I could immediately see from his demeanor that this man was definitely a military commander. Quick, penetrating blue eyes assessed me.

"As these men have said, sir, I am Jonathan Smythe, lately of Barbados, in search of my father, Thomas Smythe, and my family. I mean no harm."

"I have seen your sword before," he said as he lovingly took the machete. "Some Spanish sailors and Caribs we have encountered carried them as well. They called them machetes and used them for clearing brush as well as for fighting." He handled the machete as only a practiced swordsman could. "I do believe you, and I do know of your father. He has been parceled land in Bare Cove, a day's journey just north of here. As it happens, I will be journeying there tomorrow for the arrival of new colonists. You can join us on this journey. But first let us get you some proper clothes so that you won't be shot on sight as a Spaniard." He laughed and handed me the machete as we traveled toward his home.

A wide smile on my face betrayed my emotion. In less than a day, I would be reunited with my family—family members I had not seen in over five years. Surely this was a true blessing for a homecoming that was long overdue.

* * *

Lieutenant Holmes was as good as his word. He led me to his own small clapboard house, where he offered me a meal, clothing, and quarters for the night. After the time at sea with the Spaniards, it felt good to be housed on dry land and among fellow Englishmen. I fell asleep as soon as my head hit the straw pallet. At daybreak, I arose and, after a short meal, set off at a brisk pace northward, along with Holmes and two other men. The three men all carried matchlocks.

"Are you expecting trouble?" I was hoping the answer was no.

"You never know with the Wampanoags and Massachusetts Natives found here. They live with us peacefully enough, but some of the Algonquin bands further to the west do not like us moving into their ancestral hunting grounds and taking vacant land. They say our cattle and hogs ruin their forests, so they urge the tribes nearest to us to fight."

"I believe I saw one of these Natives on my journey here."

"You will be seeing your fair share soon enough." Holmes chuckled to himself at the thought of it.

No sooner were the words out of his mouth than we broke into a clearing in the woods. The clearing contained a collection of fifteen huts with thin wisps of wood smoke rising from small holes in the roofs. I later learned the huts were called wigwams, or *wetus*, and they encircled a red wooden pole vertically sunk into the ground and decorated with deeply carved figures and animals. This was the spiritual center of their village.

Dogs barked, and naked children scrambled into the huts. Slowly, cautiously, the members of the village crept back out from the huts. The men came out first—muscular men with dark, tattooed skin that seemed to shine on its own and long, straight raven-black hair that reached to their waists. The men were naked to the waist and wore deerskin breeches and soft deerskin shoes; dark eyes stared impassively at us. The women emerged from the wigwams next. Shorter than the men, the women had the same penetrating dark eyes and long black hair. They were also naked to the waist! I was more than a little uncomfortable at the sight of half-naked women. I had seen hints of breasts from the Native island women of Barbados but never nakedness like this before. To me, it was unnerving. The women and Holmes laughed at my embarrassment.

One of the older Natives approached Holmes; I assumed he was the leader of this tribe. He grunted something that sounded like "Wuneekeesuq." Holmes responded likewise. The two leaders then proceeded to "talk" through hand gestures. In the meantime, the women and children surrounded the other two men and me. They all admired my "big knife." I noticed, too, that the women and children all seemed accustomed to seeing the colonists and showed little fear. Holmes gave the leader a small handful of beads he called wampum and then motioned to our men that the meeting was concluded.

As we left the village, Holmes confided to me, "We just paid for passage through the Wampanoag lands with those wampum beads. Pequot heathens visited this village two days ago. They asked the tribe here to join them in fighting us and destroying our settlements. This is not good news. I must tell Captain Standish of this when we next meet. For the rest of our journey to Bare Cove, we will need to be most vigilant."

"These peoples seemed most friendly. Why would they join with these Pequots?" I was more than a little bemused by this situation.

"The Wampanoags do befriend us," continued Holmes, "but they will side with the more warlike Pequots or face destruction of their own villages from them—it is as simple as that!" With that direct answer, Holmes said no more on the subject and, with a frown on his face, continued on his way. *Could it possibly be as simple as that?* Not wanting to irritate Holmes further, I decided to not pursue the issue. The journey to Bare Cove continued for the rest of the day. I again marveled at the rich diversity of the land through which we traveled—rich earth and good drainage for crops, much timber with which to build and fashion cabins and barns, and game in abundance. It would take much dedicated work to clear and farm but not any more work than the jungles and plantation in Barbados. I was sure that my father and my brother, Jacob, would be doing well with their lands.

* * *

Dusk quickly approached as our band of men reached the outskirts of Bare Cove. Holmes understood that I was impatient to find my family, but he needed first to find the village elders to tell them of the imminent Pequot dangers. This accomplished, Holmes led me to my family's parcel.

"Good luck to you, Smythe. I hope you find your family well and prospering, but from the look of it, I would say they need some help here."

I heartily thanked him and turned toward the cabin. A small, feeble light shone from the one window of what could only be called a ramshackle thatch-roofed cabin, which was barely eight feet by ten feet. I bounded to the front door and knocked. I heard a shuffling noise inside, and the door creaked open. There, in amazement, stood my brother, Jacob. I rushed in to hug my brother, who stood back, not sure of the person in front of him.

"Brother, it is Jonathan! I have come home to you and the rest of the family!"

Jacob grabbed me and, with tears coursing down his cheeks, uncontrollably sobbed. "Please, Brother, take me to Father and the rest of the family!"

"Jonathan, there is no rest of the family. Father died this past spring from consumption, your sisters from smallpox. Mother passed before we left Badby Village. I am all you have left." His wracking sobs became gut wrenching. I had dreamed of finding my family happy and working together to build their dream in this new land, but now, with Jacob in despair, I discovered that I would need to take control over our destinies.

"Come, sit and rest yourself, Jacob; then tell me of your journey here and the progress you have made over the last five years since last we were together." I was hoping that by narrating his tale, Jacob would calm himself.

"After you left, Jonathan, O'Malley's thugs returned, looking for vengeance for the killing of their leader. We sent them off to Bristol as was planned, but when they realized that they had been tricked, Kingley's reign of terror began. He and his paid thugs made life miserable for most of the village—seized more and more of our croplands for his own uses, imposed new tithes, and then placed taxes on our looms and weaving. He took the heart and joy out of the village. After Mother passed, Father made the decision to move to the Massachusetts plantation. We arrived over two years ago now. We were not prepared for the challenges of the wilderness here. The long winters can be cold and cruel, with deep snows and driving winds. I am sure that is what caused Father's sickness and death. The girls met the same fate faced by most of the neighbors here. The pox ran through the colony like the plague it is. Most of the families here lost members. We have a sixty-acre parcel of land with plenty of timber for building. I have been struggling to plant and harvest the best I can, but I am only one person with one set of hands. There is only so much one person can do."

"You are no longer just one. Tomorrow we will start to create a plan for success here. Have you any crops to harvest?"

"The heathens taught us how to plant and harvest corn, beans, and squash. I cleared and planted about three acres of these crops. If the harvest is a success, we won't go hungry—we should have sufficient food to sustain us. The forests provide some meat from the hunt, and the bay provides fish and shellfish. We will need to work hard to store away food in our larder for the coming winter months, for we now have two mouths to feed."

"Aye, Brother, we have both faced challenges. Tomorrow we will face the challenges of this new land together, with the strength of two. It is good to be with you and good to be finally home!" Without further discussion, we crawled onto our straw sleeping pallets and soon drifted off to sleep—both of us, now with lighter hearts, murmured prayers of thankfulness.

The next morning, I roamed the Smythe parcel of land, hoping that by doing so I could quickly resolve any issues I had with the property. Just as Jacob had told me, I found the land relatively flat and rich where it had been cleared. Jacob's plantings were doing well, though they were meager. The forests held a variety of good timber and adequate game for hunting. The ocean and sheltered bay, less than a half mile from this parcel by a well-broken trail through the forest, could yield easy fishing and shellfish collection. And it looked as if a well for water could be easily had, given the small freshwater creek that ran from a pond in the forest just to the west of the cabin. It eased my mind that Father and Jacob had selected the parcel well. During the inspection, I sensed eyes watching my every move, but I could find no sign of movement. I shrugged the feeling off, telling myself it was an animal, perhaps even a wolf, or simply nervousness in a strange and new land.

* * *

The following weeks and months found us hard at work, repairing and enlarging our cabin in preparation for the winter to come. We sawed logs for the rough clapboard walls and filled any chinks with a moss-and-straw mixture; enlarged and repaired the fireplace with field stones; cut, split, and stacked firewood; and tilled and planted additional acreage. We made the decision to expand the cabin and to roof it with plank roofing shingles instead of the more common thatch. These tasks took considerable time and effort but comforted us, for we knew that the work was for us and no one else. We worked well together and made considerable progress.

No small surprise, I proved to be the better hunter. I successfully set out snares for small game and discovered a salt lick nearby, which yielded several deer for venison, and turkeys. We smoked the meat and hung it from the rafters of our cabin. The three acres of corn, beans, and squash matured well, and we looked forward to the approaching harvest. During my hunting forays into the surrounding forests, I found patches of blackberries and currants. We dried these fruits to add much-needed variety to our diets. We built a small surplus of fresh game, smoked foods, and furs, which we traded with neighboring colonists for a milk cow, a young ox, and ducks. We crafted a small barn to house our stores and the ox and cow. The ox proved invaluable for hauling, land clearing, and plowing.

Jacob steadily improved from the morose figure I had found months before. We had exchanged descriptions of our separate journeys; Jacob was amazed at my tale of misadventure on the ocean and luck at finding passage to the colony. He found my account of the island of Barbados and Uncle Richard's plantation incredible and asked me the reasons for my departure.

"I learned through Father's letter to Uncle Richard that the family was crossing to the Bay Colony here. It was my dream to reunite with the family and work our own lands, as you have started to do. Uncle Richard asked me to stay and partner with him, but I felt my life was here. I feel I am truly lucky to be here with you." I sensed that Jacob would have gladly accepted Uncle Richard's offer.

For my part, I attempted to keep Jacob from retelling the desperation and sorrow he'd experienced at the loss of our father, our mother, and the girls. It would do him no good. I easily found the simple graves of the departed family members in the burying ground near the center of the village and paid homage to them. I felt no need to linger there. They would be remembered in Jacob's heartfelt prayers to the Almighty. I fingered the carved ivory tooth containing the soil from Aaron's grave, which still hung around my neck. I pledged again that he too would never be forgotten.

As the summer days grew shorter and autumn quickly approached, I began to notice that Jacob was spending more time following Lord's Day services at the neighboring Deckers' parcel. I knew that the Decker family harbored several unmarried daughters and was curious to discover my brother's intentions. *Does Jacob intend to take a wife, and, if so, when?* I felt gladness for my brother, for I knew that he longed for the partnership of a woman in his life passage. For my own part, I felt no such need at present. Perhaps there would come a time when this partnership might arrive for me as well. I would do my best to help him in his search.

*　　　　*　　　　*

Finally, Jacob confessed in a stammering manner, "Yes, Brother, I have decided in taking a wife, one Mercy Decker, who is willing, but I have not as yet approached Goodman Decker, her father, concerning this relationship or arrangements. Would you be willing to help me approach the father?"

I was more than a little amused by the situation but agreed to help my older brother—only after we agreed on a course of action, however. That day, over the evening meal, we talked through our plan. First, Jacob would talk with Mercy Decker about her insights into the father's mind-set on approval. We both understood that we would have to post Jacob's parcel and improvements as part of this arrangement if approved by the father; Mercy Decker's dowry could be worth about half the value of the Smythe holdings, but that value was determined by the father. This type of betrothal arrangement, of course, left love and attraction to develop after the marriage, not because of it. *I, of course, will be left with nothing—again!*

"Jonathan, dear brother, I know you have lived through much and worked hard to develop this land. You have brought me back from the edge of despair to this new awakening. I owe you much, much more than I can ever repay. I—we, if Mercy will have me—would want you to continue to live here. She has told me as much. This is your home as much as it is mine."

"Brother, you have helped me as much as I have helped you. This place does feel like home to me, but you need room to begin your new family. I have been considering for some time that I would like to explore this new land further, to see what lies beyond some of these settlements and forests. But, first, let us meet with your wife-to-be and father-in-law to see what is before us." With a smile, I slapped my brother on the back, wishing us both luck.

After Lord's Day services the following week, I dutifully followed Jacob to the Decker parcel for the planned meeting with Mercy Decker and her father. The Decker family parcel was well laid out and fully planted for harvest, with ample pastures for sheep and cattle. A stout cabin and barn, both in good repair, welcomed us. Goodman Decker was an imposing figure with a full-flowing beard and commanding demeanor; Goody Decker was stout, mild mannered, and cheerful. Mercy greeted us, giving Jacob a welcoming smile, sat us at a table offering us small beer and corn bread with honey, and then hastily withdrew. I gave Jacob an approving nod; Mercy Decker was a blonde and comely young woman whom I myself had noticed at Lord's Day services.

"Jacob Smythe, you show interest in my daughter Mercy—be it so?" Goodman Decker leaned forward toward Jacob as if to physically extract words from him.

"Aye, Goodman Decker, it is so." Jacob's face became almost purple with embarrassment, but somehow he continued. "My brother, Jonathan, and I offer our parcel as commitment in this betrothal."

"What does your brother have to do with this betrothal? Do you not fully own your parcel? If that is the case, then we have no need for further words."

"I have no actual share in this parcel, Goodman Decker. I have helped my brother, Jacob, improve his land so that he can now work it alone. It is my intent to explore this colony further. He thought your daughter Mercy could be a partner in this effort, but perhaps that is not the case here." I felt my anger rising. Jacob stared at me with an open mouth.

"Son, it is not my intent to discourage a union but to clarify it with the Lord's blessings. I have seen the work you have accomplished since your coming. It is good and substantial. I have seen Brother Jacob's own improvement as well. That is also good, for we were concerned with his well-being. The improvements seem to be in most part your doing, not Jacob's. I say to you now, what is your intent?"

"If I am to be made the issue here, sir, then we are both mistaken in this matter." It was now Jacob's turn to become enraged. "I faced the loss of my entire family. My brother returned, and we have shared this work, these improvements, as a family should. It is to that family we wish to add your daughter." Jacob stood and made to leave, with me at his heels.

"Sit, my son, you have made your case and made it well. Your offer is accepted, and, God willing, we will have more additions to our families to celebrate. Let us speak to Mercy's dowry."

With that, he clapped Jacob on the back and bid us to sit. Over the course of the next several hours, we hammered out the dowry arrangement for the betrothal of Jacob and Mercy and set a date to coincide with the harvest celebrations and feasts of thanksgiving. We were pleased with the arrangements, receiving a handsome dowry consisting of several pigs, seeds for planting, and a saddle horse. We would now have a growing household, which was good—and especially good for Jacob. I knew in my heart I would be leaving sooner rather than later.

THE AWAKENING

PART IV

Chapter 7

We have heard with our ears, O God, our fathers have told us,
what work thou didst in their days, in the times of old.
How thou didst drive out the heathen with thy hand,
and plantedst them; how thou didst afflict the people, and cast them out.
Psalm 44:1–2

Bare Cove, Massachusetts Bay Colony—Winter 1635

Following the marriage of Jacob to Mercy Decker and the onset of winter, I finally had time to ponder my own future and consider options. Mercy was pleasant enough to me in the cramped cabin, and Jacob was insistent on my staying on the parcel, but I felt that nagging need to be my own man, to control my own future. Certainly it would have been easy enough to settle there, perhaps take a wife and build another cabin on the parcel, but my life experiences had changed me, as one would expect. I now believed that I, and I alone, controlled my destiny; the decisions and choices I made were my decisions and choices, not His decisions and choices. I was still a believer in the Almighty, for there had been far too many happenings in my life that I could not fully explain. Yet I felt a restlessness, an urge to continually look at the horizon or the tree line and question what lay beyond. It was a feeling I could not fully explain, but it moved me. And this feeling was going to result in moving me again. Jacob would be shocked at these feelings and would not understand, but I knew that following these feelings would lead to departure from the parcel and my family. The choice saddened me, but the future prospects lightened my heart.

But the question remains as to where the search will take me next. I had heard in the village that John Winthrop was now the governor of this Massachusetts Bay Colony. *Perhaps I could journey to this new village called Boston, meet with John Winthrop and his good son Henry, and plan from there.* It would be good to talk with Henry Winthrop and discuss the experiences in Barbados with him. I decided that the coming spring, when the weather cleared, would be the time to put this tentative plan into action.

* * *

Spring could not break early enough for me. The ice was off our pond, flocks of geese were honking north, and the early buds were beginning to swell—sure signs that nature was beginning to awaken. And Mercy was heavy with child. The time had come to announce my intent to leave and begin my own journey. Following Lord's Day services in March 1636, I met with Jacob and Mercy.

"Brother Jacob and Sister Mercy, I believe the time has come for me to begin my life in a different direction from yours. I intend to leave our home here tomorrow and day journey to Boston to meet with Governor Winthrop and his son Henry. This Henry befriended me in my departure from Portsmouth and was responsible for arranging my crossing to Barbados. I am deeply grateful to him and look forward to reuniting with him. I thank you for allowing me to be a part of your home. You have made me welcome here, and I cherish you both, soon to be three of you, but I feel that the time is right for this parting. I wish to pay for the saddle horse and a musket, powder, and shot I will need for this journey."

"Jonathan, we will give to you the things you need and want for your journey. It is because of you and your efforts that all of this happened.

You will always have a home here with us. God be with you, Brother." Jacob spread his arms out wide, and we heartily embraced.

The next morning, I began my spring travel to Boston. Uneventful it was, but the journey piqued my interest as to the possibilities. I could see that to the west a new, vast wilderness was just beginning to unfold itself. There was a challenging freshness to this land that appealed to me more every waking day.

I found Boston to be just as I had thought—a vital and growing port village. I had no trouble in finding the home of Governor John Winthrop on High Street. After hitching the horse to a nearby tree, I approached the front door to the handsome clapboard house with leaded glass windows. I knocked tentatively for admittance. A servant answered my knock and asked for my business.

"I am Jonathan Smythe, a friend of the Winthrop family. I wish to meet with your master on business."

On hearing the Smythe name, John Winthrop burst into the doorway, warmly greeting me. "Come, come, Jonathan. I see you have finally arrived here in the colony. How did you find Barbados? Come in and tell me of your adventures, for I am sure you have had some."

Winthrop ushered me into his great room to two stiff-backed chairs on opposite sides of a plank table. The room was large and contained more books piled on shelves than I had ever before seen. A fireplace with a warm, well-tended log fire completed the setting.

Over the course of the following hours and several small beers, I relayed all that had transpired since our last meeting—the voyage, indenture in Barbados, the misadventure and rescue on the high seas, my family in Bare Cove, and the travel to Boston. I was deeply saddened to learn that Henry Winthrop had arrived in the colony in July 1630 on the *Talbot* and, on the very next day while exploring, had drowned in the river that flowed through here. It was a tragic loss for the family and for me as well. Henry's wife and child were part of the family living here in this house with John Winthrop.

"Providence has surely graced you, Jonathan, and has sent you to us at this opportune moment. Let me share with you the terrible needs we have now facing our colony. There is trouble here with the Native nations in the plantations. The Natives feel that the colonists are encroaching onto tribal hunting lands and that this overall press of civilization has caused some of the heathens to rebel. It is our belief that any vacant lands are there for the taking. In turn, the Natives believe that these lands belong to no one—or, more perversely, everyone. Three powerful and warlike tribes in the southwestern part of the plantations are especially agitated: the Narragansett, Pequot, and Niantic nations. Of these tribes, the Pequots—led by their sachem, Sassacus—have declared their intent to attack us and run us out of the country. Over the past two years, their bands of warriors have killed or captured twenty-five of our fellow colonists in most heinous fashions, burning and looting farms and villages and taking prisoners of women and children. Who knows what fate has in store for these poor people? I have been charged with organizing a militia of stout-hearted men to march into the Connecticut plantation and punish these tribes."

"I heard from Lieutenant Holmes that the Pequots have already met with some of the Wampanoags just south of here," I tentatively added. I did not mention to Winthrop that Holmes had hinted that the Wampanoags might be forced to side with the Pequots in this conflict.

"Can we count on you, Jonathan, to help us with these efforts? I know my son Henry would have been the first to volunteer."

"I too wish that Henry were here with us. As I told you, I have a brother and his wife just south of here whose holdings need armed protection that this militia may provide them. I will do this fighting for them. But alas, sir, I will need provisions and arms that only moneys can purchase."

"Have no fears as to that, Jonathan. I will provide you with whatever you may need. Of course, I also offer you food and shelter here until your departure. It is settled then?"

"Aye, let it be so, good sir. But first tell me more of this new land to which I go. Are there parcels of land for settlement and improvement? Are all of the tribes as violent to the English colonists as these Pequots?"

"Good man, Jonathan! Let us first wash the dust from travel off your palate and refresh yourself; then we can talk of this journey further, and I will answer your questions."

* * *

In these talks with Winthrop, I learned much about this new land and its peoples. John Winthrop's eldest son, John Jr., also known as Winthrop the Younger, had recently been commissioned as governor of the River Colony and kept his father well versed in the latest news from that colony.

"The banks of the Connecticut River valley are lush and fertile, and the river itself provides the colonists who settle there with an easy route for the transport of goods." Winthrop was now settled into his sermon voice and continued on.

"Several large villages have been settled, including Point Saybrook at the mouth of the River. A large contingent of colonists from Newtown in the Massachusetts Bay has recently departed to establish new settlements they are calling Hartford and Wethersfield on the banks of this river. And trading posts are needed along the upper Connecticut River to increase our beaver pelt and fur trades with the Native tribes, namely the Nipmucs, Sokokis, and Pocumtucs. All of these settlements and incursions by our colonists are causing increased friction with the Native tribes, leading to the savage outbreaks of violence now witnessed." Winthrop now changed the topic to the Native tribes and the real reasons for this discussion.

"Jonathan, the Pequots and their sachem, Sassacus, have conspired against us with other smaller heathen nations," Winthrop lectured on, "including the Niantics in the Connecticut Colony, in joint efforts to force our colonists off their tribal lands. We have recently constructed a fort called Saybrook under the command of Lieutenant Colonel Lion Gardiner, a stout-hearted soldier who is now suffering the brunt of these attacks, losing several men in the process." Winthrop paused to let this information settle and then, after clearing his throat, continued his narrative.

"Captain John Endecott has been appointed commander in chief for our mission, a godly man. Captain John Underhill will be joining him. The trained militia is to sail in August from Boston to call to account the Pequot tribes for the earlier murders of Captain Stone and his crew near Saybrook and the more-recent killings of Captain Oldham and his crew at New Shoreham, on Block Island. I believe that our Massachusetts mission will be reinforced by a separate militia mission out of Connecticut soon to arrive at Saybrook Fort. What do you think of this mission now, Jonathan?"

"It seems the Natives have forced our hand with these killings. We do need to protect our families, but at what costs? And do the Natives not have claims of their own?" I could sense that Winthrop was not pleased with my questioning the motives for this mission and for seeming to side with the Natives.

"Jonathan, you are newly arrived here with little knowledge of the customs of these Natives. They are not like us. They are true heathens with no belief in God or knowledge of His teachings. As heaven is my witness, they keep more than one wife, worship the trees and beasts, and have been known to eat each other. They don't own this land; they worship it!" With that, Winthrop jumped up and began pacing the room.

"You are right, of course, sir! I only meant to humbly discover how the Natives thought of this land. Perchance I can learn more during this mission." My answer seemed to calm Winthrop from his pacing. We parted company for the evening, but I could not help feeling that there were more questions than answers to be found in this wilderness land. I now had an opportunity to discover parts of this new land I had only dreamed about exploring before. And there was the chance to learn more of these mysterious Natives. The month of August could not arrive soon enough for me.

*   *   *

Winthrop proved true to his word, providing me with food and shelter during the summer months leading up to my departure. He had my horse stabled and then returned to Jacob in Bare Cove with messages to my family as to my recruitment. Word back from Jacob that he had sired a strong son this past spring filled my heart with gladness. His farm was prospering with ample crops and growing herds. He and Mercy were happy and well, but he was cautious for my safety in this mission. He reported that colonists were arriving in constant streams, pushing the boundaries of the village and colony ever westward.

I was provisioned with armor consisting of a pikeman's pot helmet and breastplate, a matchlock musket, a saber, a shot and powder bandolier, latchet boots, and several changes of clothes. August 1636 found me ready to report for duty to Captain Endecott, who seemed a zealous but hotheaded Puritan. I heartily thanked Winthrop for his hospitality and support, and I joined the other farmer recruits for training that included formations, loading and firing our muskets on command, and other military maneuvers. I learned, as M'Gey had previously lectured and cautioned me, there was a large amount of waiting in the military.

Captain Endecott finally commanded us into formation and read the orders to the assembled militia prior to our departure.

"We are commissioned to travel to New Shoreham on Block Island, just off the coast south of Providence, where we are to engage any and all Pequot savages and take capture of their women and children. Once accomplished, we will sail to the Narragansetts and Pequots on the mainland to extract our justice for heinous crimes against us. We will ask the Narragansetts and Pequots to turn over the murderers of Stone, Oldham, and their men; demand wampum tribute to be paid;

and command that these heathens deliver women and children to us as hostages."

Is it not rather strange that we would forcibly take women and children as hostages? Military orders could not be directly questioned—at least not at this early stage of duty. Perchance the women and children were easier to capture than the ever-elusive warriors appeared to be.

Shortly thereafter, we were crammed aboard three small ships and set sail with a stiff breeze from Boston Harbor for the small bit of island offshore of the Connecticut colony called New Shoreham. As the ships dropped anchor off the island, we espied a small band of Native warriors jumping, jeering, and waving on the beach. By the time boats were filled with men, launched, and beached, most of the warriors had laughingly fled, leaving behind only a handful of warriors, whom Endecott ordered his men to summarily execute. This small number was hardly the punishment that Endecott and Underhill had envisioned. An enraged Captain Endecott ordered that the abandoned wigwams and cornfields be torched.

We returned to our boats, rowed to the ships, and set sail for the mainland. My third encounter with the Natives had been as mysterious as my first—they were there and then gone. I wondered if, in fact, this type of action was their warfare strategy—not the full, out-in-the-open style we were accustomed to in European warfare but a shoot-and-run style better adapted to the thickly wooded countryside. *If it proves to be the latter, will the militia and officers be fully prepared for it?*

As the ships closed into the shoreline of the southern Connecticut plantation on a rainy and windswept day, we spied a band of heathens and a small village on the mouth of the river named Pequot. Taking heart at the possibilities for further punishment for the Natives, Captain Endecott ordered a small mission ashore to demand wampum and hostages. I was selected as a member of this mission.

Chapter 8

Our small contingent of militia alighted from the small boats and quickly gained the shore at the mouth of the Pequot River. Just as quickly, we were surrounded by a handful of black-painted warriors. *Are they Pequots, Niantics, Narragansetts, or Mohegans?* No one seemed to know, and that included Captains Endecott and Underhill.

How is the militia to war against the right group of Natives if we cannot tell them apart? Will we not risk killing friendly Natives? Or, sadly, does it not make any difference? I had heard Captain Endecott say that it did not.

The leader of this band of Natives stepped forward, approached Endecott, and, in broken English, announced, "You English look for Sassacus, mighty sachem of Pequots. We find and bring here—you wait!"

We waited and waited, but they did not return.

Enraged with this tactic, Endecott ordered a scouting party north up the Pequot River. "Burn every heathen village you come across! Burn the cornfields and stores; kill every heathen warrior you contact!" *If we meet with Native warriors of any great number, our small band of scouts will not stand a chance.* We departed upriver as ordered.

Another young recruit, curly-haired Hezekiah Parker, and I had been selected, along with seven others. We separated into small groups and disappeared into the dense forest in different directions. Hezekiah and I headed north along the west bank of the river.

Not only did my perch on a bluff along this Pequot River provide warmth from filtered sunlight to dry my clothes, but the scrubby undergrowth also yielded me cover and much-needed shooting sightlines—protection from the eyes of the roaming bands of godless Pequot warriors I knew must be searching for me. I was armed with a matchlock, shot, and powder, but keeping the supplies dry and the musket functioning was a major task. The matchlock musket was accurate only for short distances, and it took three minutes to reload. In this dense undergrowth, I would be extremely lucky to aim and fire it with any accuracy. A pike—or, better yet, a yew bow and quiver of arrows—would have been better for the close encounters I knew could be forthcoming.

Streaks of sunlight separated the dark clouds that stretched across the river valley, filtering through the forest canopy and glimmering off the swollen whirlpools in the muddy river that spilled through this lush valley. The massive tree trunks of this primeval place were left darkened by the rainy cascades, adding to the gloom. Moisture dripped from every overhanging limb and leaf, and swirls of mist rose from the river. The rains had bestowed urgent life to this river.

No broken man-made trails were visible to me through the tangled undergrowth; only narrow animal trails descended down to the riverbank. Never before had I seen such a variety of beasts and plants in these seemingly untouched, unending, and virgin forests. But there were mosquitoes, fleas, and leeches aplenty, especially after the rains, and the mosquitoes swarmed to torment me. The wool clothing I wore was now completely soggy, offering little protection from these pests, which only added to my misery, as did the hastily cobbled and soaked shoes. If only God had seen fit to provide me and the others with good, tough boots to keep our feet dry and free from rot. I luckily possessed a beaver-felt slouch hat that kept the mist and pests from my head. I had left the armor on board the ship. The blessings of God would be sorely needed on this mission to help us face the challenges of unknown weather, unknown wilderness, and the fierce savages who inhabited it.

Hezekiah signaled me with a wave from his scouting position

down along the riverbank that he was settled in. Suddenly, Hezekiah stopped waving and excitedly jumped up, bringing his matchlock to firing position.

"Heathens!" His screams echoed through the forest.

I gaped in horror as I witnessed the attack. He was beaten again and again with wooden war clubs wielded by three black-painted, muscular, and half-naked savages. The blows rained down on the head of the now-defenseless Hezekiah. Blood gushed from the wounds. Just as suddenly, the skirmish was over. Fiendish war screams echoed along the river as the band of Pequot warriors dragged Hezekiah into the dense surrounding forest, to what fate I could only assume.

I thanked God for my own salvation. There was no hope of rescuing Hezekiah from the savages, and God knew how many more were part of this war party. My best hope for escape was to remain quiet and motionless, attempt to meet up with the other scouts, and report back to Captain Underhill. If Hezekiah were still living—and that was doubtful, given the severity of the beating I had just witnessed—he might be tortured and then killed for information regarding the numbers and locations of soldiers sent on this mission. Only God knew what the tortures would entail. As Winthrop had told me, and others in the militia had agreed, the Pequots had been known to eat their captives. And they would be back, searching in earnest for me.

I nervously checked and rechecked my shot and powder, knowing full well that I would only get one shot off before I was overwhelmed. The machete given to me by my uncle, which was slipped safely into my belt, might end up being my final defense.

Slowly rising from the hidden position, I knew that the time had come to attempt to flee. A twig snapped behind me. I whirled to face my supposed attackers, losing my balance. Falling backward, I slid headfirst down the embankment and into the river. The water was shockingly cold. I went under!

Choking and gasping for air, my flailing arms hit a floating tree limb in the fast-moving river. I grabbed fast onto the limb with both hands, keeping my head just above water and struggling to find my musket with my feet—no easy task in this silt-filled torrent. The musket had vanished.

I kicked off my shoes, holding tightly on to the limb with one hand and steering the limb with the other. The river, now in flood, was chocked with debris. The current in the river was strongest toward the far bank. I cautiously kicked my way through the floating debris and toward the opposite shore. The tree limb carrying me began to move swiftly downriver.

I realized that the main body of soldiers under the command of Captain Underhill was encamped next to the mouth of the river south of here. If I could hold on to this limb long enough and float downriver, I might reach the safety of the ships and encampment to report the skirmish with the Pequots. I had to reach them, but it would not be easy. The icy water quickly soaked my woolen clothes. I now clearly saw both of the riverbanks and, looking back upriver, spied no pursuit.

My arms and legs quickly lost feeling. Struggling to hold on to the lifesaving tree limb, I began to lose track of time and seemed to hopelessly float forever. As the river rounded a long bend into the small bay mouthing out to the sound, I spotted the small rescue encampment and began waving frantically to attract attention. One of the sentries spotted me and ran for help. I knew if I could get my legs working, I could reach the shore.

A rope smacked the water just out of reach to my right. I let go of the tree limb and kicked toward the rope. My icy hands grabbed the rope as best they could, desperately struggling to hold on as the soldiers dragged me ashore. I attempted to right myself, but my frozen limbs did not obey. Losing consciousness, I slid back into the muddy river.

I awoke to a warm fire and a sip of brandy. Regaining consciousness and warmth in my limbs took some time and effort, but I soon felt well enough to stand. I would need dry clothing, shoes, and a musket to rejoin the efforts here. I soon was resupplied and ordered to help reload the boats.

We discovered several small fishing camps near the river mouth that appeared to have been recently vacated. The simple huts, made of bent poles with bark and grass coverings, were easily torched. Several hapless warriors were captured and beheaded by pikes wielded by two of the militia. We finally headed back to the safety of our ships with our grizzly trophies, no booty, and no prisoners.

* * *

We journeyed by ship westward; with a good breeze, it was only a day's sail to Saybrook Fort, at the mouth of the Connecticut River. Our arrival was heralded by much fanfare, as the militia barracked there had been under siege by the Pequots for some time and our forces were sorely needed. We staked the grizzly trophy heads on the palisades as a warning to all Natives in the area. Lieutenant Colonel Lion Gardiner, the commander of the fort, seemed not well pleased with this exhibition of Native executions ordered by Endecott. He believed the fort would now face the upcoming winter months with swarms of vengeful Niantic and Pequot warriors roaming the forests nearby.

Captain John Mason from Hartford had floated down the Connecticut River, armed with his commission, and arrived at Saybrook Fort with a band of hastily trained militiamen. At the outset, Colonel Gardiner and Captains Endecott, Underhill, and Mason all seemed to have their own reasons and understandings on how to further proceed against these Pequots. Also now at the fort, the Mohegan sachem, Uncas, and his band of fierce Mohegan warriors sought fidelity to the English force. They were sent by Gardiner in a sortie against Pequots in the area. Uncas, tall, battle scarred, and great in strength, returned with more heathen heads, which were added to the collection on the fort's palisades. *But are these Pequot warrior heads?* The members of the militia did not seem to either know or care. Our officers took Uncas at his word. The Mohegans had passed the test.

I began studying the Mohegan warriors at the fort and took considerable notice of their dress, mannerisms, and weapons. They all carried stout bows and full quivers of bronze- or flint-tipped arrows; most also wielded stone-tipped clubs, iron knives, and deadly looking hatchets. They dressed simply in leather breechcloths, leggings, and shoes they called moccasins. Their partially shaved heads glistened with raccoon grease, with the remaining narrow band of hair greased to stand up front-to-back and fashionably festooned with colorful feathers. Several of the heathen warriors shaved their heads in a different manner, leaving long topknots of hair, called scalp locks, that they braided and let fall down the backs of their heads. Their war paint was black or blue covering part or all of their faces and chests. Their overall appearance was one of fierce preparedness. I could see that these true warriors were trained from an early age in the art of thick-forest warfare; they had the ability to glide through the thickest of underbrush without making sounds, appearing and reappearing at will. We had heard that the savage Pequot warriors were even more skilled and formidable in this type of warfare than these Mohegans—not good news for our poorly trained farmer militia from Hartford and Massachusetts Bay, even with the promise of musket firepower.

I befriended one Mohegan warrior in particular. Taller than the other warriors, he seemed to smile more and looked open and friendly. Instead of a stone-headed war club, this warrior carried an intricately carved, wood-handled ax fashioned with a large, extremely sharp flint head—one of the most deadly looking battle axes I had ever seen. I learned through trial and error and rough attempts at sign language that this strange ax had been handed down from father to son for many generations. He called himself Qaqi Muks, or Running Wolf; he preferred to call me Big Knife after my machete. It seemed easy for me to learn the common hand sign language the Natives used to communicate between tribes, and I found it useful in discovering information and learning about some of their customs. Not surprisingly, Running Wolf learned about the English language and customs from me. As it turned out, we were both apt students.

With the harsh and snow-filled winter weather closing in, the Pequot tribes continued to lay siege to the fort and carefully scouted the comings and goings of everyone and everything in it. Sorties were sent out to confront the marauding Pequot war parties with little success. On several of these sorties, I learned from Running Wolf some of the tracking techniques, food sources, and survival techniques that he was willing to share. The winter snows helped me to more easily learn to follow the tracks of the common game animals found here. The militia quickly settled into the working routines of military encampments: commands, close-order drills and formations, and weapons maintenance.

* * *

Spring 1637 broke early and wet, with dark clouds racing inland from the sound to our south. Running Wolf warned me, "Big Knife, Niantic river tribes join Pequots. No like farmers on river and lands."

Supply boats from Hartford relayed to us that Sassacus had listened to the pleas from these tribes to act, for in April 1637, a war party had been sent upriver to a settlement on the Connecticut River called Wethersfield, just south of Hartford. They had surprised the colonists there, killing most of the settlers and their cattle and horses and escaping with two young women captives. All of us were enraged by this news, especially news of the two captive women. We had heard that the Pequots could be brutal to their captives, and our imaginations played havoc with us. We prayed during Lord's Day services for the safe release of all captives, especially these young women.

I had become close friends with Running Wolf, and we daily exchanged information and gained deeper understandings of each other's culture and beliefs. For my part, I began to develop a deeper understanding of the rich Mohegan life and their spiritual connections to their surroundings. Running Wolf developed a grasp of English, albeit broken and sometimes with laughable pairings of words and phrases. My stumbling attempts at Algonquin and Mohegan also brought smiles on his part.

Through these understandings, I soon came to believe that the Natives of related tribes must share these same beliefs, these same relationships with nature and wildlife. If this were true, I felt I would be hard-pressed to kill Natives who were simply protecting their homelands. I did know, however, that I did not wish to suffer the same sad fate as Hezekiah Parker—and I would defend myself.

Our friendship was not welcome to the rest of the militia or to the other Mohegan warriors. Mistrust was common to both sides. I hoped—and I was sure that Running Wolf felt the same—that we might somehow bring our peoples together through mutual understandings. We were to learn soon just how wrong we both were.

THE KILLINGS

PART V

Chapter 9

Yea, they shall not be planted;
yea, they shall not be sown:
yea, their stock shall not take root in the earth:
and he shall also blow upon them, and
they shall wither, and the whirlwind shall
take them away as stubble.
Isaiah 40:24

Saybrook Fort—May 1637

Preparations now neared completion for our first major armed offensive against the Pequot nation. Gardiner had sent some of Mason's untested militia back to Hartford, north up the Connecticut River, replacing them with some of his own trained militia, who joined the combined militiamen under the commands of Captains Mason and Underhill. The Mohegan sachem, Uncas, commanded some eighty Mohegan warriors. Three ships arrived at the mouth of the Connecticut River, near the fort, to carry us to the landing point, which was still as of yet unknown. Captains Mason, Underhill, and Gardiner were still in dispute as to how to carry out this first militia movement. Our weapons, arms, and supplies were at the ready. The Mohegans seemed prepared to fight.

We noticed in our scouting trips through the surrounding forests that the Pequots appeared to have pulled back to their villages, or the warriors were massing at one key location.

"Pequots have two forts—Weinshauks on Pequot River. Sassacus is sachem there. Mamoho, sachem of Missituc fort on Mystic River. Protect east. No Pequot warriors here. No good for us!" signed Running Wolf. No, this did not portend well for us, for it seemed that the Pequots were massing their forces for a spring offensive.

As the month progressed, the weather became warmer and more favorable for movements by our militia. The captains requested divine direction for this mission, and this direction must have been positively given, for, finally, the word was given to board the three ships in the harbor. Ninety-five of our militia and eighty Mohegans, along with armaments and supplies, were tightly packed aboard the three vessels, and we set sail. Running Wolf and I departed on separate ships, for our militia was not allowed to travel by ship with the Mohegans. Narragansett was the port we sailed for. We also learned that Gardiner had made the decision not to travel with us but had sent some of his trained fighting men and his chirurgeon, Dr. Pell.

Fair winds and fairly calm seas pushed us eastward past the green-forested coastline; three good-sized rivers mouthed into the sound along our journey: the Pequot, the Mystic, and the Pawcatuck. We figured two of these rivers housed the Pequot palisade forts. No one in the militia seemed to know for sure. We sailed onward for two days and dropped anchor off Narragansett but did not land, remaining content to wait offshore for Lord's Day services. That night, dark clouds, rain, and strong winds blew into the sound, forcing us to pass the night and the next day attempting to keep our powder and supplies dry and our stomachs quiet. The stomachs of our Mohegan brothers did not fare as well on the tossing ships. All were thankful when we disembarked and again found ourselves on firm, somewhat-dry land.

Captains Mason and Underhill met with the Narragansett sachem,

Miantonomo, and requested passage through the Narragansett lands to attack the Pequots from the rear flank.

Running Wolf cautioned me, "Miantonomo no like fight against Pequots—many more Pequot warriors. Good to attack Weinshauks by water boats." This advice made sense to me and would take great advantage of a quick attack.

Our captains, Mason and Underhill, thought little of Miantonomo's advice and refused to wait for Captain Patrick's three ships soon promised out of Massachusetts Bay, along with additional militiamen and much-needed supplies. Instead, they further reduced our numbers by fifteen men, ordering them to wait at the Narragansett fort with the ships and Chirurgeon Pell, who also refused to journey farther on this mission. Reasons were not given for these decisions, nor were reasons to be expected.

*   *   *

The weather cleared, and the morning brought bright sunshine and commands for us to move westward, guided by our Mohegan allies. Running Wolf signed to me that some of the Niantic and Miantonomo's braves might be joining us later. We marched westward through dense forests, thickets, and swampy lands. Without our Native guides, we would easily have lost our way through this dense and unknown land.

There was a trail to follow, but we could not march abreast and followed each other in single file. This stretched our force out and increased our chances for attacks. With our supplies, arms, and armor, this passage across the numerous streams and small ponds was proving to be difficult. Several feet to either side of the trail, we faced thick underbrush and shrubs, which provided excellent hiding places for Pequots to launch spears and arrows at us. Some of the militia began to feel the effects of the heat on this march; we needed to stop for rest.

We reached the Niantic fort of the sachem Ninigret, who came out to meet us as we approached. He seemed friendly but did not allow us to enter his fort. An enraged Captain Mason ordered us to block all exits from the fort. If we could not enter, no one could leave—at least, that was what he believed. *In the dark of night, how can we tell who enters or leaves?*

Running Wolf signed, "Pequots know we come. Know we here. No good for us." We rested and spent an unsettled night.

We arose the following day and continued our march westward toward the Pawcatuck River. As we approached the river, we followed the trail that turned north where the river narrowed to find an easy ford. The forest and underbrush were still thick on either side of our passage. Uncas warned us that this easy ford was also a frequent fishing spot for the Pequots. We stopped to uneasily rest at the ford, expecting an attack. None came. We soon found that the Niantic and most of the Narragansett warriors had deserted us and returned home. Most of the militia wanted to do the same, since it was obvious to us that this mission was neither secret nor quiet. Even the farmers in the militia knew that there was no possibility of surprise now. We pressed onward to the Mystic River from this spot.

Captain Mason ordered that we could not make the journey that day to the major Pequot fort at Weinshauks; instead, we would march onto the Missituc fort of Mamoho. We rested and counseled there and then slogged our way west through swampy land and the quickly approaching nightfall.

As the skies cleared and the full moon rose, we forded the Mystic River and approached tall, rock-strewn hills, which provided us with ample protection for our evening rest. Sentinels were sent out to guard our repose. They reported singing and chanting from the Pequots at the Missituc fort. The commotion continued throughout the night, but our bivouac gave us sound rest from our day's rigorous march.

Well after daybreak, we arose to bright sunshine and brief prayers to continue our mission. Our Mohegans guided us to a path that they said would lead us directly to the Missituc fort. We proceeded along this path, which skirted the Mystic River on our left, heading south, deeper into Pequot territory. We traveled around and into one bay of this river and into another and, finally, approached the hill where, according to our Mohegans, the Missituc fort was located. *Why are there no Pequots standing guard here at the noisy approach of eighty militiamen and scores of Natives?* We looked to our remaining Niantic allies for advice and found that, supposedly terrified, they had also deserted us to the rear.

Captain Mason disdainfully ordered the Mohegan warriors to stand off at a distance and watch how well the English fought. Running Wolf signed, "Mohegan no make war on old men, women, and children." For myself, I hoped I would not be forced to make that decision. *What did Running Wolf mean by "old men, women, and children"?* We were now left to our own devices.

* * *

The assault began. Matchlocks and swords at the ready, we charged up the hill in two columns, past the Indian cornfields and lodges, and reached the summit of the hill. We came upon a very large clearing and a circular palisade fort encompassing some sixty to seventy dwellings. This fort was larger than most of the English villages I had seen in the Massachusetts Bay Colony. The quiet was ominous. We saw no Pequot sentries, and only a few campfires still smoked. I saw nothing moving inside the fort but heard a cry of "*Owanux!*" (Englishman). A solitary dog barked.

Mason screamed, "Ring the fort!" Our meager forces encircled the palisade, spaced several fathoms apart.

"Ready to volley!"

Then Mason barked again. "Fire!"

We fired our matchlocks in unison, or nearly so, into the fort. The roar of the guns was deafening. Splinters of wood from the wooden stakes in the palisade flew everywhere. Gun smoke filled the air. Not surprisingly, our crossfire volley killed two of our militia outright, as the circular compound forced us to fire directly into the fort and at our unlucky opposite number.

Captains Mason and Underhill separated the militia into two groups of twenty men each and directed them to the two entrances to the fort to continue the assault. The remaining forty men ringed the palisade and entrances to provide support for the assault militia and to be at the ready to staunch the flow of Pequots supposedly fleeing the fort. Our Native allies provided little, if any, military support and sought the shelter of the surrounding forests.

I followed Captain Underhill to the nearest entrance. Chest-high brush densely crammed into the entranceway blocked our passage. We worked hard to clear it. Then, single file, we forced ourselves inside and into the fort. We found empty wigwams and nothing else.

Suddenly, a barrage of arrows assaulted us, fired from among the wigwams. It raked us, wounding several. We saw no attackers but heard the sudden war cries. We reloaded our matchlocks and fired on command into the wigwams and at shadows. These volleys must have killed several Pequots. My musket misfired, but I had no time to reload, as stout Pequot warriors attempted to rush past us, forcing hand-to-hand fighting. Captain Mason's men faced the same blocked entrance but met with little initial resistance. Most of the Pequot warriors we faced in the fort were killed by slashing swords and pikes. I faced no one, for, just as suddenly, there were no more Natives left standing.

"Fire the wigwams, and flee the fort," ordered Mason. The rush roofs of the wigwams torched easily, and the flames quickly spread. The Missituc fort was now a mass of heat, flames, smoke, and confusion. The bodies of several dead Pequot warriors littered the ground inside the fort. We left as quickly as we could, dragging our own dead and wounded with us. This part of the battle seemed to end as quickly as it had begun.

Once outside the fort, I observed that most of our remaining men were tending to our dead and injured. I sought Running Wolf to learn about the escaping Pequots.

"No time worry. Pequot warriors now come!"

"Who was in the fort then?"

"Old men!"

We assembled our remaining militia and trekked southwest down the hill. Carrying the dead and helping the wounded drastically reduced our abilities to fight, for we now were a much smaller group of healthy militia. Mason ordered a few of our Native allies to help us move our dead and wounded. We reached a brook at the bottom of the hill and paused to rest and refresh ourselves.

Suddenly, we faced a hoard of screaming and enraged Pequot warriors who came rushing down the hill toward us. Matchlocks were fired in volley, wounding some of the warriors and forcing the rest back up the hill and into the surrounding forest. The Pequots again rushed us as we attempted to reload. Swords and pikes replaced the now-useless muskets as the fighting became intense and, again, hand to hand, man-to-man. The thick brush provided the Pequots hidden locations from which to unleash their arrows. Several more of our militia saw the effects of these ambushes.

Suddenly, two strong Pequot warriors leaped out of the brush and grabbed at me. I could do little to defend myself. A stone-headed war club wielded by one of the warriors crashed violently into my helmet. I staggered and went down. My world went black.

* * *

I awoke to a throbbing head. It was now nightfall and eerily quiet except for the chirping of crickets and frogs. Through my blurred vision, I saw that I was covered in leaves and brush. I started to cry out, but a hand closed over my mouth. Running Wolf! I attempted to rise, but he roughly forced me back down.

"Rest. You need strength."

"Where is my militia? Where am I? Are they safe? Am I safe?"

"We talk later."

I closed my eyes, and the darkness again surrounded me.

Soaked to the skin, I awoke to a bright morning. It must have rained during the night as I'd slept. Slowly, I began to move my limbs, which were stiff from inactivity and dampness. Running Wolf noticed my movement, brushed off the leaves and brush, and helped me sit upright. I was not sure at all where I was. He brought me water to drink. My head still pounded and ached from the war-club blow as my memories of the battle and ambush slowly returned. I still needed to know my situation.

"Soldiers?"

"Go to boats. Pequots go to Weinshauks. I bring you here. We go to Mohegan Shantok two days. You be safe there."

I could not believe all this had really happened—the assault on the Missituc fort; the killing and the flames; the running battle with the Pequots; and the dead, wounded, and dying. Patrick's ships out of Boston must finally have arrived with supplies and additional militia. I discovered that I still had my matchlock, shot, powder, and treasured machete. Neither breastplate nor helmet had survived the previous day's skirmishes. I was sure that the helmet had been dented beyond repair, given the large and tender swelling on my head.

As soon as I could stand and walk without passing out, we could leave and begin the journey. Running Wolf offered me some dried meat, which he called pemmican, to eat. The water, the pemmican, and the bark of the willow tree he told me to chew refreshed me and numbed the head pain so that I slept through a full day. By early the following afternoon, I felt well enough to travel.

Running Wolf set a steady but easy pace along a well-worn path northward. The trail ran through the thick forests and low hills. We stopped and rested at nightfall and ate a frugal but nourishing meal of pemmican mixed with berries that Running Wolf had harvested along the trail. It felt good to be up and moving again. The clean and fresh smells of the pine forests refreshed me and buoyed my spirits. I noticed clear signs of recent moccasin travel north along this trail—Mohegans, Pequots, or both? Running Wolf was silent on this matter.

We awoke at sunrise, broke camp, and crossed the headwaters of the Pequot River into Mohegan lands. The Shantok fort of Uncas was now less than a half day's travel through these forests. As we headed west, we passed a small camp used for fishing and several recently planted cornfields.

I would be allowed to meet the family of Running Wolf; his two sisters, wife, children, and father, a brave warrior, still lived as the Clan of the Wolf in this village. I was more than a little hesitant about my welcome at the village.

"You no worry. Mohegan not same as Pequot."

For me, that was good enough, but I was filled with mixed emotions. *Am I really a prisoner of the Mohegans? Did Captains Mason and Underhill count me as missing, dead, or a deserter?* I was sure I would find out some answers from the Mohegans soon. These thoughts running through my mind worried me most.

* * *

We quickly approached the outskirts of a village containing ten or so wigwams. The larger Shantok fort of Uncas was close by, but the dense forest obstructed my view of it. Dogs and children came running to greet Running Wolf but fell back when they noticed my presence. Suddenly, Mohegans were everywhere, clamoring and welcoming Running Wolf back to his village. He motioned for me to follow him as he led me to the center of the village, where several elder Mohegan warriors had gathered.

"This Másqisut Muks" (Red Wolf), Running Wolf said, nodding to one of the elder warriors, "my father." His father stared impassively at me. "This sachem of village, Sákák Ôkatuq" (Gray Cloud). He reacted to me the same as Red Wolf had. Next, Running Wolf pointed to me.

"This Big Knife." This introduction generated a reaction: they stared intently at my machete hanging from my belt. I could not resist a slight smile.

"Big Knife injured in battle against Pequots and needs time to heal on his journey." Running Wolf looked to both Red Wolf and Gray Cloud for any signs of agreement and, seeing none, continued. "He will bring honor to our village as a friend of our sachem, Uncas."

Gray Cloud slightly raised one of his eyebrows and then signed, "You welcome, Big Knife, to village. You rest here on journey."

With that, I realized that although I had received a welcome to stay, it was not for long. My presence in their village might be noticed by the other villages or by the Pequots, and there could be difficulties. It would take some time for my head to fully mend and for me to make plans about my future direction, but for now, I could safely rest.

Running Wolf and I left the elders for his family's wetus on the outskirts of the village. Here I met his wife, son and daughter, mother, and two sisters and shared a meal of succotash and pemmican. His oldest sister, Ásuwanuw (Cornsilk), smiled shyly at me, welcomed me, and brought me my meal. Of medium build, she was obviously a mature young woman, with warm eyes. Her golden skin glistened as she moved with nubile grace. Immediately enchanted, I felt my face reddening. I was not accustomed to feeling this way around any woman, English or Native. We exchanged sly glances throughout the rest of the meal; I would find her staring at me, and as soon as she saw me staring back, she would look away—a visual, entertaining game of flirtation. It brought a smile to my face, which was reflected in hers.

They dressed me as one of them, with deerskin leggings and moccasins. I felt the freedom of this new world. I reveled in this freedom, and this did much to lighten my mood. I thought that Running Wolf must have known long ago, or what seemed long ago, at Saybrook Fort that I would be open to his world. That was why he'd spent the time teaching me about his world and why he'd hidden me during the assault at the Missituc fort. I owed him much, my new brother, for that was what he was becoming to me. Over the next several weeks, I became more accepted by the Mohegans as a welcome visitor in their village.

Over the course of my stay in their village, the Mohegans taught me much about the forests and wildlife, including their spirit worship of their surroundings, in which the life they came in contact with had spirits of its own. I found this embrace and worship of their surroundings not only refreshing but also a reflection of my own life experiences. This life in the village enjoyed a natural cadence with the nature and wilderness that surrounded us. We hunted, fished, ate, and lived in natural harmony.

News of the continuing English and Pequot skirmishes filtered back to us. I learned that the English forces had shipped their dead and wounded back to Boston and the Bay Colony. The combined forces of Mason and Patrick had marched through Pequot territory back to Saybrook Fort, torching everything as they progressed. I cared little for this news, now having learned that most of the Pequots had found safety and shelter with the Mohegans, Niantics, and Nipmucs. It made sense that the Pequot warriors and their families would be absorbed by their brother nations, where they had family relationships. Most members of these Native nations seem to be blood related, and Running Wolf had told me as much.

I began to form an idea about building relationships between the English and the Native peoples by running a trading post on the Connecticut River to foster fur trade and, hopefully, trust among our peoples. The Massachusetts colony and England clamored for the furs of many game animals, beaver being the prime pelt. The Natives had their own desires for firearms, blankets, pans and pots, and tools of all sorts. It was a thriving business opportunity. This big Connecticut River was a good source for transport of goods, with easy access to the northern tribes and fur-trapping areas. Running Wolf agreed to give his help and hands to this plan. I also knew that this venture would require me to work as both an Englishman and a Native in order to trade the bartered furs and receive trade goods from the Dutch and English.

We thought it was a good plan. However, I needed some moneys to start this trading business—I thought perhaps my brother, Jacob, or Winthrop might be willing to invest. I needed to travel back east to find the funding and make arrangements.

I now felt recovered enough to journey to Saybrook Fort to report back to the militia officers there about my injuries and healing. Running Wolf agreed to guide me. From there, I could possibly arrange transport back to the Bay Colony.

My plans for the trading post were ready and well laid out. With Running Wolf's help, I was able to draft barter guidelines for Native trappers. The moneys required to start this business were small but more than I had in hand. A partner would be necessary—one who would not be directly involved in running the trading post but could be relied upon to purchase pelts from us and provide us with barter items. Profits from the sale of pelts could be split on agreed terms between the partners. With these basic plans, I felt I could approach a worthy partner. It now remained for me to discover this partner and move the plans forward.

Chapter 10

The day arrived to set out for Saybrook Fort. Running Wolf took leave from his family, and we left after daybreak and traveled west from the village toward the Connecticut River—a journey of several days. Running Wolf hoped to find a village willing to lend a canoe to make travel to the fort easier and safer. At the end of the third day, we arrived at the river and searched for a village. Because of the militia activities against the Pequots and the activities of unfriendly colonists along the river, we found the Natives less than friendly to Puritan Englishmen. Running Wolf was, however, able to bargain with them for the use of a canoe, so we set out on the river leg of our journey. I proved to be more than a little awkward in handling the unstable vessel but, with Running Wolf's guidance, soon gained some basic mastery.

The distance rapidly slipped by as the great tidal river pushed us southward toward Saybrook Fort. I was eager to be reunited with members of the militia but even more eager to find funding for my new endeavors. *Will it be possible to seek out Colonel Gardiner for advice?* He seemed to be the most knowledgeable on Native relationships and possessed a good understanding of the politics commonplace to the region. I assumed I would also need to report back to Captains Mason and Underhill to explain my absence to them.

The majestic, forest-covered hills gave way to flatlands and scrubby brush as we approached the mouth of the river. As we rounded a large bend in the river, the palisade of Saybrook Fort came into view. We pushed the canoe to the western bank and climbed out. Just as quickly as we set foot on the bank, sentries grabbed us and rushed us into the presence of Captain Underhill.

"So back from the dead, I see." Underhill seemed far from pleased to see me.

"Only by the grace of God and the shelter provided by a Mohegan warrior. After the burning of the Missituc fort, I was overpowered and clubbed by two Pequot warriors. Running Wolf hid me from them and gave me shelter near the Mohegan Shantok fort. As soon as I was able to travel, I sought out his guidance to return here. I owe him my life."

"Fair enough—we will permit you to rejoin the militia and continue with our noble efforts against these damned Pequots. As you know, we vanquished the Pequots at their Missituc fort and continued our march to Weinshauks and burned their fort there. We are now hunting them down wherever we can find them. You are timely to join us in this mission."

"I come here on a different mission. I wish to return to Boston and the Bay Colony to seek business and financial guidance from the Winthrops."

"I do see that as a possibility, but perhaps Captain Mason and I might come to an understanding with you in regard to your travels. We have noticed that you seem to have developed an understanding with the Mohegans here. We seek a deeper understanding of their tribal relationships—Mohegan to Pequot to Niantic to Narragansett—instead of relying on their smiling utterances and pretended obeisance. Your role could be as mediator between us and the heathens to better military efficiencies. Do these works for us over the next several weeks as we plan and execute our continuing campaign, and then we will release you to Boston and the Bay Colony. What think you of this role?"

Taken aback by this offer, an offer to work among the Natives to help further understanding and relationships, I was also more than a little hesitant about the couching of Underhill's terms. *Would I be ordered to take advantage of my friendships with the Natives to points of betrayal? I need some time to think through this offer.*

"I thank you for the offer, Captain. I will need some time to consider."

"Very well. Report back to me tomorrow morning!"

I turned and left without further word. I found Running Wolf near the Mohegan encampment.

"My friend, I think we may have been offered an opportunity of a lifetime. Underhill has offered me the chance to work with the Mohegan sachems and our militia to gain a better understanding of the tribal relationships. Once I have mastered this task, they will release me to Boston so I can find moneys for our trading post. Is not this great news?"

He simply shrugged as we walked back toward the militia quarters.

* * *

"You are very lucky, lad, that the heathen didn't take your hair, throw you on a sharpened stake, or roast you alive over a fire," said one of the more vocal militia members as I entered the small, cramped barrack. A chorus of well-wishes and welcomes resounded through the barrack. Many of these simple farmers were survivors of the Missituc fort campaign and heartily glad of my survival as well.

"These damned captains prance around like they know what they're doing, but none of them do—running through the forests without a damned notion in their heads. It is fortunate that we're not all heathen meat—to hell with Underhill and Mason!" This same member wanted to say more but just shook his head and, grumbling to himself, sat down. Most of these men were eager to return in one piece to the Bay Colony and their loved ones and their farm plots, which by now sorely needed tending, but did not want to tempt being accused of heresy or banished from the colonies because of offenses to these politically favored officers.

Again I told of my salvation by my Mohegan brother and my safe return. Many of these men found it hard to believe the amount of trust I had placed in a Mohegan warrior. For my part, I could not doubt their mistrust after having witnessed the wounding and deaths of comrades during the recent campaign, but this outburst of mistrust signaled the types of reactions I would be facing should I accept Underhill's offer. I needed to talk through this offer further with Running Wolf to gauge his reactions and advice. This meeting would need to take place that night.

Searching for Running Wolf in the Mohegan camp outside the fort, I happened to come upon Colonel Gardiner, who was standing and looking across the river to the east.

"It's Smythe, is it not? Glad to see of your return to our meager forces."

"Aye, saved by the bravery of a Mohegan ally. I owe them much. In fact, just today Captain Underhill offered me a position of mediator between our forces and our Native allies." My positive response generated a small smile from Gardiner.

"That be so, is it? We have noticed your understanding of the Mohegans and the other Natives here. This is good, for we should all strive to understand their customs and ways without trampling them. However, I take not much stock of the motives of Underhill or Mason. As for the Niantics, the Mohegans, and the rest of these tribes, you would do well to talk to Uncas firstly. He has more knowledge than most give credit for."

Throwing caution to the wind, I broached my trading-post plan with him.

"Another good thing! Perchance you will need a financial partner. I could see myself in that role, for this Pequot matter is sure to end sooner than later, and we will all need sources of income and further plans to move forward. I would suggest a spot several furlongs north of Hartford, just recently settled by a man named Pynchon. Agawam, I believe it is named. It is close to an area on the river further north named Nonotuck.

You'll find falls in the river just north of Hartford that limit further ship traffic northward, fertile land, and, better yet, ample opportunity. Once you have completed your tasks for Underhill, search me out again and we will talk further."

We parted company, and straightaway I eagerly sought out Running Wolf to tell him the good news. I did not relish the idea of traveling to the Bay Colony on bended knee to my brother, Jacob; his father-in law, Decker; or the Winthrops. I was no longer the naive young man who had fled from Badby Village trusting in Providence. My years of servitude in Barbados and in the militia had hardened me and forged in me a solid belief in self; I now possessed a freedom to make my own choices in opposition to the unbending Puritan teachings. This change in me made life decisions like these much easier. Here, I faced an honest and forthright man with whom I could easily work, who knew the areas, and, better yet, who had an appreciation for the Native tribes. I could not have found a better partner. I found Running Wolf just outside the Mohegan encampment.

"I work with Underhill and sachems for short time. I tell Underhill tomorrow. I talk to Gardiner about trading post. He think Nonotuck good."

"You talk Uncas first. More honest. Nonotuck in Nipmuc and Pocumtuc lands. It not far from Mohawk trail—that good!"

"We talk more tomorrow."

* * *

I did not sleep well that night, as my mind turned over and over the plans and details. I would need to work with Underhill and the Native sachems to learn their participation and their concerns. The first sachem to talk to was rightly Uncas, who could point me to the right Natives to talk with concerning their plans and opinions. This might just work with a little work and polish.

The next morning, I reported to Captain Underhill, as he'd requested.

"Captain, I accept your offer to work with the Natives as your mediator agent over the course of the next several weeks or until you find you no longer need my services. We have not discussed pay for these services, but I am willing to begin that conversation now if you so desire."

"Good, Smythe!" Underhill shrugged his shoulders and did not seem overtly positive about this assignment and the acceptance. "As for pay for your services, since you are not true military and do not carry military rank, you are not allowed pay. But I did have conversations with Captain Mason and Colonel Gardiner last night and learned of your desire to build a trading post north of Saybrook Fort and Hartford. Is this true, Smythe?"

"Aye, sir, it is. I talked briefly with Colonel Gardiner, and he encouraged me to it."

"Since that is the case here, perhaps we can work out an arrangement where we can help you get started with your trading post. It would be in our military interest to have a trusted person such as you, with knowledge of the Natives, in an informative position on the outlying areas of the colonies. Do you understand our concerns and meaning here?"

"Aye, Captain, I do. It would be an honor to report to the commissioned military and the governors of these colonies in such roles. Again, sir, I accept both offers."

"Good man, Smythe. For now, see to Uncas, and learn what you can about where the Pequots are headed and how we can put an end to this heathen campaign."

Running Wolf had little to add to the conversation that we'd had the previous day, but he was glad that our trading-post plans looked as if they could be moved forward. I had seen Uncas before the Missituc fort campaign and on our march to that fort. He was an impressive sachem; he was large and muscular, with piercing dark eyes that noticed every movement, yet he had an air of command and wisdom. He directed his warriors with strength and knowledge. He would be a good source of information if he sensed I could be trusted. My mission focused on earning that trust.

Running Wolf ushered me into the wetus of Uncas. I found he was seated cross-legged on a mat, seemingly deep in thought. I had brought Running Wolf with me as an interpreter but quickly discovered that Uncas spoke and understood English well. Once we progressed from the introductions, I broached the reasons for the visit.

"Uncas, sachem of the Mohegans, I come to you at the request of Captain Underhill to discover the latest locations of Sassacus, sachem of the Pequots, and his warriors."

"Cannot the great Captain Underhill himself come to me with this request?" Uncas did not seem pleased that a mere militiaman would come to him with this request, and from his tone, I gathered that he did not possess much respect for Underhill.

"Aye, he could have come himself, but he is now busy in preparing new plans for the campaign against Sassacus. He has sent me as his special friend and as a brother to Running Wolf, son of Red Wolf." I hoped that mentioning my friendship with Running Wolf might help to bridge the relationship and further trust.

"Yes, I know of the Mohegan Wolf clan of brave warriors. If you are a brother to this clan, you must be a brave warrior yourself." The hint of a smile creased his weathered face. "I will tell you what I know of Sassacus of the Pequots. Sassacus and a large band of warriors and families crossed the Connecticut River, heading westward just north of the fort here, killing several Owanux on the journey. We can track the journey, for his large band. They seek the safety of Dutch country, but we must act quickly!"

"I understand you, Uncas, and the need for action. I will relay this news to Captain Underhill in all haste. I thank you for your words and sincerity, and I look forward to talking with you again."

With a brief nod, Uncas stood, and I understood that the counsel with him was over. From a pouch tied to his waist, Uncas pulled a belt of wampum, beautifully beaded in a fashion I had never before seen. He extended this belt to me.

"Big Knife, take this belt of peace with you. It will give you safe passage through the lands of our brother tribes as a friend of the Mohegans, as a trusted friend of Uncas."

This unexpected gift was the trust for which I had earnestly searched; this brief meeting had produced the means for working with the sachems of important tribes. Running Wolf and I were both pleased as we exited the wetus in search of Captain Underhill.

* * *

"Good, Smythe, we will marshal our forces and chase these heathens down. Captain Mason will be in command of the militia and Mohegans now here at the fort in this mission. We will move to action in all haste!"

The next day, we departed by vessels and skirted along the coast westward for three days, hoping by this transport to quickly overtake the Pequots and catch them unawares. We saw activity onshore that proved to be other Natives. We landed finally, and Captain Mason ordered our Mohegans to scout the exact location of the Pequot band.

The band of scouts soon returned and reported to Mason.

"We find Pequot at Sasqua village. Warriors and families hide in swamp."

This Mattabesic village was located on a small hilltop, with the swamp close by at the foot of the hill. Captain Mason ordered our militia forces to encircle the swamp. One of our militiamen, a fur trader named Jameson who knew the Pequot language, and I ventured into the swamp, calling out to the Pequots to surrender.

Out of the dense brush jumped two Pequot warriors. Holding up the wampum belt of Uncas, I signed for peace. This action halted their rush toward us. These warriors captured us and roughly dragged us to a swamp clearing and into the presence of their sachem, Sassacus.

What a difference between Uncas and Sassacus! In front of me was a fierce-looking monster of a man covered in black war paint—a sachem who ruled by brute force. Immensely muscled, he pushed through his warriors surrounding him and stuck his brutish face into my own.

He signed, for he knew little English, "Why you come here, Owanux? You wish to die?"

I gulped and replied, "Let us take Pequot families now to safety. Your warriors surrender later."

"We no surrender to Owanux! Take our old men, women, and children with you! Pequot warriors ready to fight!"

"So be it!" I answered, not knowing what the results would be. Soon, a struggling mass of Pequot families collected at the clearing. Sassacus allowed us to leave under guard. There was no trust here at all. This sorry mass of humanity followed us back through the swamp to our militia position. Captain Mason made the decision to hand over the families to the local Mattabesic.

Sassacus and his warriors remained in the swamp and continued to fight us into nightfall; the action was hectic and violent. The thick underbrush in the swamp again became an ally to the Pequots, making them almost invisible to us. The militia volley-fired their muskets at the slightest rustle of brush, wounding several of our own men and killing only a couple of Pequot warriors.

At daybreak, Sassacus and his remaining warriors repeatedly rushed our defenses, finally breaking through our encirclement and escaping. The Mohegan scouts told me that Sassacus had led his warrior band north, seeking safety in Mohawk country. Again Sassacus had escaped the wrath of the militia, and we could accomplish little else there, so we reloaded our vessels and departed.

* * *

We returned to Saybrook Fort to lick our wounds and regroup. I took this opportunity to seek out Colonel Gardiner to discuss our mutual interests. He found it interesting that Underhill would offer anything, let alone a business opportunity such as this one.

"Be careful, and keep your wits about you. My offer of financing still stands on solid ground," warned Gardiner. I heartily thanked him and rejoined the militia and Running Wolf.

We spent the next month talking over and finalizing our plans for the future. We heard from Uncas that the scalp of Sassacus and the severed heads of several of his warriors had been sent by the Mohawks to Governor Winthrop in Hartford. How anyone knew the trophies were the scalp of Sassacus and the heads of Pequot warriors was a question that no one cared to answer. In September, we were ordered to Hartford for the treaty council. I looked forward to heading north up the Connecticut River to scout the area for trading-post locations.

The council at Hartford doled out most of the surviving Pequots among the Mohegans, Narragansetts, and Niantics. A covenant was signed that stated that the Pequots could never again inhabit their lands or be called Pequots. The Mohegans at the council told me that this covenant made no real difference, as a large number of the Pequots had already been absorbed into their brother nations. Those Pequot souls unfortunate enough to be delivered into Puritan hands became the true tragedies, for they became slaves in the colonies or were shipped in servitude to Bermuda or the Caribbean.

With the treaty council concluded, Running Wolf and I journeyed northward. The land north of Hartford was as promised—lush and fertile. One William Pynchon of Roxbury had purchased land called Agawam from the Pocumtuc and Nipmuc Natives and begun his farming and trading there. If Running Wolf and I could meet with Pynchon, I felt he might prove to be the best partner yet, for we had learned that Pynchon believed that dealings with the Native tribes should be on friendly terms. As luck would have it, when we reached Agawam, we found the recently arrived Pynchon busily settling in by staking out plots of land for his groups of soon-to-arrive colonists. We discovered him to be the type of man we had envisioned—aggressive, shrewd, loyal, and knowledgeable in the fur trade. Settling down in his rustic cabin, we proceeded to lay out the proposal for our trading post.

"You and your Native friend here have selected well for the site of your trading post further north up the river to Nonotuck. A site up there will bring to you fur trade from tribes even further to the north, to the east, and, yes, even to the west, in the surrounds of the Dutch Albany. Native paths and trails cross and crisscross throughout this northern territory. Nonotuck is a good location. And your friend, a true Native, is a good asset to have in this trade. He will provide trust to the other Natives." Pynchon nodded and beamed his approval.

Running Wolf and I agreed to ship our bartered pelts down the Connecticut on his small river shallops or canoes to his warehouse just south of Agawam. He, in turn, would buy our pelts and provide us with barter goods, which we could then float upstream to our post on the river. He also laid out for us the types of barter goods he would provide for us— cotton cloth and shirts, blankets, iron knives, mirrors, combs, gunpowder and shot, axes and hoes, and some meat products. Besides the much-sought-after beaver pelts, we could expect to barter for otter, mink, marten, raccoon, woodchuck, and fox pelts; bear skins; the occasional deer or moose hide; and even feathers. In addition to barter with the Natives, he proposed that we also think about barter with the influx of farmer settlers and colonists. Their barter needs were similar to the Natives', with the addition of necessary forged items, such as plowshares, shovels, saws, nails, and axes. Pynchon told us to stake out the land parcel we wanted, and since we were now in business together, we could pay for the land in proceeds from our barter trade. We sealed the offer with our marks on a parchment contract he provided, with handshakes all around.

THE SOWING

PART VI

Chapter 11

Be not deceived; God is not mocked:
for whatsoever a man soweth,
that shall he also reap.
Galatians 6:7

Shantok Fort, Connecticut Colony—Fall 1637

It was not that I had forgotten the arrangements with Underhill and Gardiner, but word had it that Underhill had returned to Boston, banished for blasphemous activities, and moved to New Netherland. Gardiner, for his part, moved to Long Island. Captain Mason still exerted influence and his style of Native warfare in Connecticut and Hartford, causing the Natives to become even more unfriendly. In fact, Pynchon and Mason had caused no small amount of turmoil with their separate viewpoints on that subject; so I was now left to my own devices, conscience, and decisions.

Following our meeting with Pynchon and the scouting of a claim in the Nonotuck areas during the early fall, we returned to Running Wolf's Mohegan village in the Connecticut Colony to spend some time with his family and winter over. He seemed a little hesitant to leave the familiarity of his surroundings, but he realized that he needed to obtain leave of his father and other relatives. His wife, Winged Heart, and his children were faithful to him and would follow his lead. I now had the opportunity to reacquaint myself with Cornsilk, the sister to Running Wolf. We had spent some fleeting moments together the first time we had met during meals and daily activities in the village, but the forthcoming winter and spring seasons could allow our relationship to blossom.

I found this tall, comely Mohegan maiden to be truly enchanting. Her long, silken black hair was woven into a single braid down her back. Her face radiated an innocent, healthy glow, yet her mischievous dark eyes slyly hinted at the mysteries of her people. Her soft deerskin leggings and shirt whispered every move of her young, womanly body. She led me on daily hikes into the surrounding forests, pointing out the tracks of small game, the places for berry picking, the best spots for fishing and wild-rice harvesting, the occasional deer, and how and where they planted and harvested their crops of corn, beans, and squash. During the worst of the winter snows, she taught me the basics of the Mohegan language, the secrets of Mohegan cooking and food storage, the making of clothes, the building of wigwams, and the social structure of their village life. I, in turn, taught her as best I could the rudiments of the English language and about some of our customs. Her understanding of English would prove to be crucial, the customs not so much. We enjoyed our days together, combining the best of both worlds. I was—we were both—truly in love.

The days spent with Cornsilk turned out to be the happiest days of my life. The tranquility of the forests, the filtered sunlight, and the harmony that these people lived in with their surroundings allowed me to exist outside of my troubles, to stand outside of myself, to see myself as I was. I had become so close to these Mohegan people that I began to wonder if I could ever leave them.

On a moonlit night, Cornsilk quietly came to my wetus and whispered to me. "I come to you of my own choice. I am yours if you want me." Her smile, the warmth of her body, her touch completed me.

"I do choose you, Cornsilk," I mumbled, half out of my mind with desire. The moon was our only light, but it seemed to completely fill our surroundings. I slipped her buckskin covering from her shoulders and gently let it fall to the ground. I struggled to remove my own clothing as our lips met. Our fingers roamed our bodies as we pressed passionately together. I gently lowered her to my sleeping pallet covered in furs. She pulled me to her and gently placed me inside her. Our rocking motions increased in rhythm until the moment of complete surrender to each other. We lay together until dawn. I was content with her by my side. It was a night I would never forget.

The morning sun cast a new light on our relationship. We had made the decision to be together, but it was not an easily accepted decision and would need the approvals of Running Wolf, Red Wolf, and, more importantly, Gray Cloud and the Mohegan village. Obviously, I was not a Mohegan, although I did feel like a member of this family and village. I felt more content there with Cornsilk, Running Wolf, and the village than I did with my brother, Jacob, in Bare Cove. Cornsilk had other suitors, who would not be pleased with her choice of an Owanux. As an Englishman, I would be cast out for boldly taking a Native as my wife, although there were some Englishmen who secretly had Native women as mistresses. A declared marriage simply would be neither allowed nor recognized in any Puritan congregation or village. I noticed evil eyes among several young warriors in the village and did not wish to cause more conflict there. Cornsilk told me that Running Wolf favored me and that he'd promised to talk to their father, Red Wolf, on my behalf.

The days turned into weeks and seemed to drag by with no word. I knew that Running Wolf had approached his father and talked on my behalf at the village council, but still there was no word of approval.

Finally, Cornsilk came to me with a smile on her face.

"Running Wolf tells me that Red Wolf and Gray Cloud, the sachem, approve marriage. Running Wolf, Winged Heart, and Red Wolf agree for sponsors." We clung to each other with true joy.

With much ceremony, our marriage was celebrated in the early spring of 1638. Cornsilk and I did not have a church as I knew one, so we used the surrounding forest as our chapel: the sky as the roof, the earth as our foundation, and the forest around us as the walls. A circle of stones became our altar. The entire village turned out for the ceremony. As we entered the marriage circle of stones, we received a gift of sacred tobacco. We cleansed and purified each other, for when we left this circle, we would become reborn as married people—not just to each other but also to the family and the Mohegan village. Cornsilk's sisters carried baskets and handed them to us, symbolizing the care for each other we brought to our marriage. Gray Cloud stepped forward to offer us a blessing, welcoming us into the Mohegan family. Running Wolf signed me the blessing of Gray Cloud.

"Now you feel no rain, for you shelter each other. Now you feel no cold, for you warm each other. Now you no more alone, for you companions for each other. Now two bodies, but only one life goes before you. Go now to your wetus; enter into the days of togetherness. May your days be good and your lives long."

I felt truer words had never been spoken. Cornsilk's sisters gave us a tied blanket, symbolizing the joining of our lives. We were to carry it with us. We were both very happy.

I thought back to the marriage of my brother, Jacob, and the happiness that surrounded Jacob and Mercy's union. More than two years had passed since we'd last seen each other, and I greatly missed them. I wished that his growing family could be present at this happy occasion. Their absence tinged my happiness with trifling sadness. Cornsilk noticed my mood, pressed her hands to my face, and whispered her love. It touched my heart and melted my gloom.

Suddenly, a thought came to me as clear as the daylight now before me. I had stumbled into my own thin place! I could see everything with extreme clarity, a spiritual clarity—a sense of oneness with my surroundings, with my new wife and life. I was in awe of everything around me in a way that revealed this place, this time as it stood before me, simple and unadorned. I was free at last! *Thank you, M'Gey, wherever you are!*

The gaiety of the marriage and village celebration lasted into the evening. In the morning, we would leave for Nonotuck and our future. That journey would begin with the packing of goods, foods, and weapons.

The village gave me a hatchet, a spear, a bow, and a quiver of arrows—all of these gifts I could readily use. Cornsilk and I prepared our own packs and rendezvoused with Running Wolf, Winged Heart, and his two children to begin our journey to our new home.

Running Wolf and I had previously staked out sites for our trading post and home cabins. We planned to travel by canoes upriver to Hartford, portage the canoes around the falls just north of there, and then continue upriver to Agawam. We would meet there with William Pynchon to finalize details of our arrangements and pick up additional supplies and some barter goods, and then we would head north. We needed to build our cabins before the onset of the winter snows, but with many willing hands, we believed the hard work would proceed at a goodly pace. We left our Mohegan family with happiness in our hearts, for we enjoyed our freedom and our future before us.

* * *

Twelve full moons had passed since Running Wolf and I were last upriver to Hartford for the treaty council and beyond to Agawam, and we now found rapid growth of Puritan colonies along this river. It was a good sign—we had chosen well the site for our trading post. After several days of paddling fully laden canoes, we passed Hartford and overnighted just north of there. Most of the colonists thought it strange to see an Englishman, one dressed as a Mohegan, with a squaw. I cared little for what they thought as long as they did not force their beliefs or menace any of our small band of travelers. Just north of Hartford, we approached the falls, which blocked easy advance upriver. Here, we portaged the canoes and supplies and reentered the river just short of Pynchon's large warehouse. The float trip on to Agawam was short.

"Halloo!" Warm greetings floated across the shining river from Pynchon, who stood on the shore as our party of canoes rounded the bend in the river into Agawam. No doubt, word of the progress of our strange band of travelers must have preceded us. As we clambered from our canoes, we introduced our families to Pynchon, who, for his part, neither took notice of nor made any comments on any of our relationships.

"Let us settle our affairs in my cabin, and then you and your families can join me in a meal," offered Pynchon. We proceeded to his cabin to complete our dealings, which were as we had proposed the previous year and agreed upon.

"I will ship your barter goods upriver to you," declared Pynchon, "just as soon as you have given me notice." He continued, "I will give you title to those acres of land you have staked out and will deduct payments for this land from the sale of your bartered and shipped pelts. I earnestly believe that our barter businesses will grow and mightily prosper." We shook hands all around and, with much heartfelt joy, joined Pynchon in a family meal. It was good to see all of us happy and contented. Our families rested that evening, with plans to continue our journey north up the river to Nonotuck the following morning.

The spring morning broke fair and clear—a promise of a good day to start our trip upriver. Pynchon rewarded us with several sharp axes and two good saws to help in the felling of trees and the building of our post and cabins and sent us on our way.

We made steady progress on the river and, in two days' time, reached our staked-out plot along the eastern shore of the river, directly opposite a large bend. We quickly offloaded our canoes and stacked our supplies securely under cover. Cornsilk and Winged Heart quickly set to work, constructing temporary wigwams to shelter us during the building process. The timbers we had felled and stacked to dry the previous year were now ready for working. Running Wolf's children—his son, Wolf's Tail, and daughter, Smiling Sun—searched the surrounding woodlands for small game, berries, and kindling. We did not let his children roam too far, for we knew not what dangers lurked in these woodlands; children made choice captives for most warring Native tribes. Running Wolf briefly scouted the area and found a large Pocumtuc village not far off—friendly or not, we did not yet know.

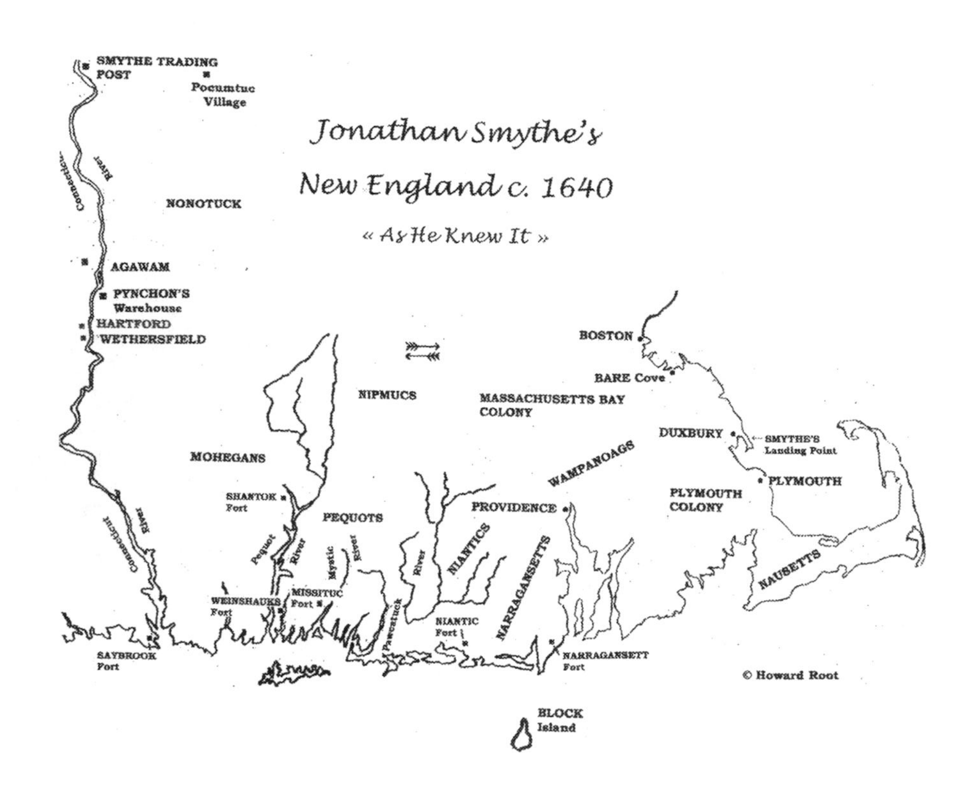
Jonathan Smythe's
New England c. 1640
« As He Knew It »
SMYTHE TRADING POST
Pocumtuc Village
Connecticut River
NONOTUCK
AGAWAM
PYNCHON'S Warehouse
HARTFORD
WETHERSFIELD
NIPMUCS
MASSACHUSETTS BAY COLONY
BOSTON
BARE Cove
DUXBURY
SMYTHE'S Landing Point
PLYMOUTH
PLYMOUTH COLONY
WAMPANOAGS
MOHEGANS
SHANTOK Fort
PEQUOTS
PROVIDENCE
Pequot River
Mystic River
River
NIANTICS
NARRAGANSETTS
NAUSETTS
WEINSHAUKS Fort
MISSITUC Fort
Pawcatuck
NIANTIC Fort
SAYBROOK Fort
NARRAGANSETT Fort
© Howard Root
BLOCK Island

Chapter 12

Smythe's Trading Post, Nonotuck—1640

For the first years of our venture, we saw our trading business steadily grow and prosper. The cabins and buildings were well constructed and in an excellent location for trade and resupply along the river. Running Wolf's family occupied a cabin that contained several rooms and was large enough to give them ample space. My separate cabin boasted a great room and separate room for sleeping quarters. Both of the cabins contained rough-hewn wood floors.

The life for our families there was good—the rich soil along the riverbank provided us with a bounty of corn and vegetables. Plentiful fish from the river and game from the surrounding forest gave us all the meat we needed, but we imported a small flock of ducks for eggs and some additional meat. We built a small landing area for canoes and dockage for handling the larger supply vessels from downriver. True to his word, Pynchon supplied us well with inventories of barter goods.

The actual trading station was a notched log blockhouse set back some distance from the river's edge in an ever-enlarging clearing. We had spread word through the surrounding Native villages as to the location of our post. Natives found their way to our post along the Native pathways that also extended farther to the west and north, into Iroquois tribal areas. As our stores of high-grade pelts filled our blockhouse, we floated them down by canoe to Agawam and Pynchon's warehouse. Running

Wolf and I supplied Pynchon with upward of four hundred fur pelts per month over these first years. And some colonists farther downriver regularly bartered portions of their crops for our forged tools and nails, although not as frequently. With a little consistent luck, we realized some good moneys and freedoms—freedoms from wants and from bigotries—and provided well for our families. I relished our independence here.

The Pocumtucs visited our trading post on a regular basis and, for the most part, seemed friendly toward us, thanks in no small part to Pynchon's policy of honesty and openhandedness with them. These tribes knew that they did not have to fear our encroachment on their domain other than our small acreage and that we wished to impose no governance over them. The fact that my Mohegans existed here as my full and equal partners—Running Wolf in our trading post and Cornsilk as my wife—offered full testimony of my honesty to our Native brothers. Running Wolf and I regularly visited their villages and found them tolerable, peaceful neighbors. We prospered. We lived well and good, with a steady pace of growth for our trading business. For the first time in my life, I felt I was fully living my life on my own terms.

* * *

In the year 1645, Cornsilk gave birth to our first child, a boy we named Aaron; he was strong and healthy, with Cornsilk's dark eyes and my curly hair. I hoped to teach him the best ways and customs of both our backgrounds so that he could face his future with open eyes. I watched with a parent's fascination the growth of this child, seeing some of myself in his movements at play and his expressions of wonder at the wild world around him. He appeared to sense his surroundings as his mother's family did. That was good, for he would need to rely on those senses to survive.

I had sent letters to my brother, Jacob, in my own cramped handwriting, informing him of my prosperity in Nonotuck and the birth of Aaron, inquiring about, in turn, his own news. I had received no reply thus far. I wondered how well Jacob was facing his own future with his wife and perhaps several young children.

Aaron, for his part, reveled in his childhood freedoms, running and playing with Wolf's Tail and Smiling Sun and exploring the fascinations of the surrounding forests. He enjoyed a strong and natural attraction to his cousins, especially to Wolf's Tail, who became more like an older brother to him. He copied Wolf's Tail's every move and action. Cornsilk, of course, adored him, for she saw in him both reflections of my background and the natural rhythms of his Native family.

* * *

Aaron, as he grew and flourished, understood and spoke in both his mother's Mohegan and my English languages, using the sign language to his advantage. He watched with the intent interest of a child the comings and goings of the Pocumtucs and other traders who traveled to our station post, including the bartering of furs for goods, and he learned a great deal about the types and grades of pelts and their values. He had a good head for the fur-trading business at a young age. Wolf's Tail took the task of teaching Aaron tracking and hunting skills in the surrounding forests. Aaron was a good pupil and a fast learner. One late summer afternoon, Aaron came running into the clearing with a small bundle of fur.

"Look, Father! A red squirrel pelt! I caught and skinned myself! It is worth something in trade, is it not?"

"Aye, that it is! Good lad! You could double your trade should you bring me another!" I smiled, for red squirrel pelts were high-quality pelts for ladies' garment and hat trims, and Aaron knew as much. Off he scampered, back into the forest, in search of Wolf's Tail and his traps. I knew he would now double or triple his catch. It was a great learning experience for him, and Wolf's Tail enjoyed being the teacher.

Our life prospered. There was a mutual and overflowing happiness among and between our families. My relationship with my true love,

Cornsilk, also grew. I could not have imagined my life without her, and I knew she felt the same. The peacefulness of our surroundings and the natural rhythms of the lifestyle magnified our commitments and bred contentment. Running Wolf and Winged Heart, we understood, felt the same, even though they did miss the Mohegan village life and their extended families. On several occasions, and for special rituals that were important parts of that life, Running Wolf's family, including Cornsilk and Aaron, returned together to their village to reunite and rejoice with their Mohegan clan. I remained behind to continue our trading activities in their absences. I missed them but knew they were safe with Running Wolf.

I missed my brother, Jacob, and his family. I pondered ways to reach out to him but had little or no success. I hoped that he was doing well. I knew that the Decker family, especially Goodman Decker, would provide shrewd guidance and governance for him.

CHAPTER 13

Smythe's Trading Post, Nonotuck—Fall 1650

Each late fall, before the river fully iced over, Running Wolf and I usually made our last float trip for the season downriver to Agawam. We had made numerous trips downriver over the past years, but our upcoming trip promised to be the most profitable. At last count, I found we had six hundred high-quality beaver pelts and a goodly mix of four hundred other furs, including marten, mink, and fox.

"Pynchon like our furs!" Running Wolf smiled and pointed toward our heavily laden canoes. "We fill three canoes! More pelts come."

"Aye, it is good," I replied, "and good for our families. Will your son be able to handle one of the canoes by himself?" I did not want to have our wives piloting one of these canoes on a trip downriver.

"Better than you!" He laughed at that and motioned for his son, Wolf's Tail, to join us. Almost as tall as his father, Wolf's Tail had grown into a strong, vital young man. He could easily handle the canoe, but I wanted to be positive of Running Wolf's agreement. For his part, Wolf's Tail seemed to be looking forward to this adventure down the river and the honor of stepping forward to assume his manly duties. Cornsilk and Winged Heart seemed less positive in their thinking. I did not know if their concerns stemmed from their maternal natures, or if they instinctively knew more about the dangers downriver than they were willing to tell me. I did know that they had faced some rebuffs from some of the Puritan colonists they'd met, but these were matters I could not control or change.

We shoved off in our loaded canoes at daybreak the next day and began our leisurely float trip downstream. We anticipated that the trip would take us two days of paddling. There was no reason to rush, as the warm fall sun and colored foliage made the paddling a pleasure. The great river pushed us easily southward. We nosed ashore at Agawam at midday on the second day of our journey and found Pynchon overjoyed in his greeting.

"Smythe, you and your partner have exceeded my expectations for your barter post. Excellent, excellent indeed! We will get a count of your furs and settle our accounts, but first let us enjoy our good fortunes." With that, Pynchon pointed toward his cabin, now a fine clapboard house with leaded glass windows, and then sat Running Wolf and me down to a table of meats, breads, and small beer. I instructed Wolf's Tail to watch over the counting of our pelts.

"Since we last talked, the fur trade has increased, and my business here has increased at a good rate. You, Smythe, and your partner here are playing no small part in this success. You will be rightfully rewarded!" One of his workers entered with a count on our fur pelts and looked at Running Wolf and me with a smirk. He handed the accounting to Pynchon.

"Even better than I originally thought, Smythe!" With this, Pynchon waddled to his desk and seemed to become preoccupied with writing and figuring. He returned forthwith with an accounting and a bag of coins. As he jiggled the bag of coins, he said, "Yes, indeed—better than I originally thought. Here's your accounting and share of the profits. You'll notice I reduced the profits by the agreed property mortgage and your cost for barter goods. Even so, I think you did handsomely!"

As I hefted the bag of coins, I nodded in agreement and smiled at Running Wolf. We'd worked hard and had prospered well as a result. I intended to share equally with him in the rewards, although he had not much use for English money.

"A word of caution for you, Smythe. I've received warnings about activities west of here. The Dutch have begun to monopolize the fur trade with the Mohawks along the Hudson River. We may need to look hard at our efforts with tribes further to the north. They've also been selling firearms to the Mohawks. There are rumblings among the Pocumtucs that the French have allied themselves with the Algonquin and Huron peoples against the entire Iroquois nation, Mohawks included. A full war will break out sooner than later. The French in New France to the north of us are relatively quiet for now, although war parties of any kind won't be good for our business."

This was not good news. Although our isolation provided some safety, we were really defenseless. A war party could burn us out or worse, and we'd have no hope of rescue. We'd have to flee—by canoe, if possible, or by foot into the surrounding forests.

"I had no idea matters could be this bad," I mumbled. "What do you think we should do?"

Pynchon shrugged. "Keep a close watch on the friendly Pocumtucs around you. They should warn you of any uprisings or war parties on the trails. Other than that, pray to our God for salvation and guidance."

I shakily stood. "We'll continue our fur trade as we have done and keep close counsel with our friendly Natives, as you have said. I do seek additional quantities of powder and shot, though, as stock against raiding parties. I cannot believe that any harm will come to us! We'll plan to return with more furs. I thank you for your counsel as well, William Pynchon. We threaten no one, nor do we seek salvation! Come, Running Wolf, let us see to your son!"

Running Wolf and I quickly returned to our now-empty canoes and found that Wolf's Tail was nowhere in sight. We found three of Pynchon's motley workers lounging on the dock near the canoes, including the head worker, who had brought in the fur count to Pynchon's office.

"Have you seen a young Native boy about here? He was watching you taking account of the furs," I anxiously said to the head worker.

"Aye, we did see the young heathen, but he gave us cheek, so we sent him on his way," said one of this crew.

"Cheek!" I exclaimed. "What mean you by 'cheek'?"

"The heathen bastard said we didn't know how to count," grumbled the head worker. "We couldn't stand for that, now could we? 'Specially from a heathen! The last we saw, he headed for the warehouse."

Running Wolf and I turned and ran for the warehouse barn, where Pynchon stored his pelts. Laughter from the workers on the dock flew after us. We found the warehouse piled high with furs and barter goods. Not a soul in sight.

The rear door of the barn was slightly ajar, so we pushed it fully open. There, dangling by the neck from a strong limb of an oak tree, was the body of Wolf's Tail, severely beaten and hanged. With a loud moan, Running Wolf quickly moved toward his son and cut him down. He tenderly held him and attempted to clean the blood from his face. Running Wolf turned his face to me, and I saw the sorrow and desolation in his eyes.

I felt rage building in me—the same rage that had consumed me after my friend Aaron's murder. I turned and ran to Pynchon's office, smashed through the door, and confronted a startled Pynchon. He hurriedly stood up from behind his desk with a puzzled look on his face.

"What in the Lord's name is the problem, Smythe? Have you lost your mind?"

"Your workers have killed Running Wolf's son out of hate and ignorance! I come now for retribution!" With that, I ran from the office, pulling my machete from my belt as I ran. Waving the machete above my head in a full circle, I charged headlong into the group of workers still standing on the dock. With savage downthrusts, I hacked at any body parts in front of me. The workers were startled by my enraged charge.

I offered them no mercy. The head worker, who now bled profusely from the stumps of both of his arms, quickly crumpled and fell from the dock into the river. Another worker was now headless. A third worker turned and began running for his life. That life soon ended by a savage blow to his head from Running Wolf's ax.

Pynchon had now arrived at the dock, huffing and puffing from exertion. "Smythe, you have killed my workers. No, it is not possible! How have you committed such depraved acts and sins? Surely we could have found God's justice through some other means!"

I could clearly see that Pynchon was thinking of his own soul and possible outcomes in the community and not mine. "An eye for an eye" was all I could mumble, for I was still shaking with rage. Then the words poured out of me. "This young man was good and honorable. He'd harmed no one. Yes, he was a Native, but he did nothing to deserve this. I'd call this fair justice from my own hands. Blame, if there is any, is mine! We'll leave now and hear no more of it."

I placed a hand on Running Wolf's shoulder and turned him toward the warehouse. We left Pynchon standing there with his mouth agape. We needed to clean the body of Wolf's Tail and wrap it for burial, but not here. We would return to our trading post and bury him there. Together, arm in arm, we walked to the body of Wolf's Tail to begin wrapping it for transport. We needed to hurry, for we knew not the extent of the alarm from the Puritan community that would most likely follow the deaths of Pynchon's workers. We would not be able to safely withstand an enraged mob of Puritan colonists.

We kept to task and, with loving care, placed the wrapped body of Running Wolf's son into one of the canoes. Pynchon, for his part and by himself, had loaded one of the canoes with the requested stocks of powder and shot. Without so much as a glance back, we glumly departed company, knowing this trip to Pynchon's Agawam might have been the last.

THE REAPING

PART VII

Chapter 14

For if a man think himself to be something,
when he is nothing, he deceiveth himself.
Galations 6:3

The trip upriver was not nearly as leisurely as the trip down, for we found the current strong against us, and we were weighed down with heavy hearts. Three days after leaving Agawam, we nosed ashore at our familiar dock and, with silent tears, unloaded the body of Wolf's Tail to the shrill screams and tearing of hair of Winged Heart and Cornsilk. With fluttering hands and uncontrollable tears, the two women recleansed and purified the body and rewrapped it for burial. Aaron was beside himself with grief at the loss of his friend and brother—so much so that he ran off into the forest. We knew that he would not go far but respected his grief and let him mourn. He returned the next morning, a sad-faced and changed young boy at five years old.

We chose Wolf's Tail's favorite spot along the river for burial. Following Mohegan mourning rituals, we buried him in a prone position on a mat of sticks, with his head pointing southwest, paralleling this section of the river. His bow, arrows, and knife were buried with him. After filling in the grave with damp soil, we piled the grave mound with river stones. Running Wolf, Winged Heart, Smiling Sun, Cornsilk, and Aaron stayed at the gravesite, chanting in Mohegan fashion for two days. I respected their grief and mourning and gave them their space and solitude.

During such times of sorrow, I found it comforting to think over my own life—the twists and turns, the happenings, and especially the changes in life that placed me on a different path, a changing passage. So it was on a warm fall day, the second day following the burial, that I sat by the river, deep in my own rambling thoughts.

I considered the passages that had brought me here to this place. My early childhood in England had not been easy. My father had been a taskmaster—out of necessity, as I saw it now. We had worked hard and long, the necessity arising from harsh tenancy conditions. Mother had been a dear and caring soul for all her family and raised us children, with a firm hand, under the Puritan teachings of strict and unquestioning obedience to the will of God as set forth in the Bible.

Then there was my resentment at the harshness of these teachings. I could not fathom the reasons behind the requirements for strict obedience, for I had mentally freed myself from these covenants at an early age and continued to reject them even now. If I had learned anything in my journeys through life, it was that I, and I alone, controlled my destiny through the decisions and actions I planned and carefully took. This awareness had carried me through the servitude in Barbados, the days of desperation on the open ocean, and my time in the militia.

My thoughts then turned to my brother, Jacob, his wife, and his growing family, and I wondered how they had prospered over the past years. I had received no word from them; perhaps they thought I had perished in the Pequot battles. I would have thought word of my safety would have reached them from some of the returning militia. I would truly enjoy seeing Jacob again.

The will of God and His providence do not control my life or my choices and decisions. This may be blasphemous, but blasphemy be damned! I made the decision to wed Cornsilk, a Native, and have a son with her. I made the decision to come to this place to run a trading business here. All of these decisions were good and well-founded decisions. This is my thin place—my place for freedom—and a good place for us. It is my glimpse of heaven on earth, and I am satisfied with that explanation. Where was God's Hand in any of these decisions? Do I deceive even myself with these thoughts?

My reverie was broken by the snapping of a twig. There stood Running Wolf with a bemused look on his face; I realized I might have been thinking these thoughts out loud. He grunted in agreement, and we began to talk about our next steps here. He was a good friend—in truth, more like a brother to me. I would have done anything for him, and him for me.

"We need scout Pocumtucs and trails. May be trouble," whispered Running Wolf. He spoke quietly, for he did not want to alarm the women.

"Aye, I agree. We should start as soon as you are able, for I am ready now," I responded. I did not desire to push Running Wolf to action during his mourning.

"We no wait. We go tomorrow, first light." Running Wolf grabbed my hand and wrapped his strong arm around my shoulder. His eyes burned with a fierce light I had not seen before. I knew that he sensed the forests and changes to them better than I.

"Yes, let us make ready and tell the women of our trip."

"We no worry women. We tell them go on hunting trip."

I agreed that Running Wolf's caution was good.

* * *

We prepared the women well with two muskets and additional powder and shot, telling them this precaution was due to tracks we'd discovered nearby from a pack of roaming wolves. Both Cornsilk and Winged Heart had been taught to load and shoot well with the muskets, and the sturdy trading-post blockhouse would provide them with ample protection should they need to seek refuge. Perhaps we were being overcautious, but Pynchon's warnings about war parties could not be lightly taken. And then, too, we needed to consider Puritan colonist reactions to the violence that had occurred in Agawam. Our hastiness to scout the surrounding area might prove fortunate if we uncovered that the warnings we had received were correct.

We pushed off in a single canoe at dawn, as planned, having loaded the canoe the prior evening with the necessary provisions. We paddled northward up the river to find a point to hide the canoe in brush by the river. The closest Pocumtuc village was to the east of our trading post, but scouting for Mohawks might find better success on trails north along the river. We struck one of the trails, with Running Wolf in the lead, and found no marks to cause alarm—no recent or frequent passages of bands of warriors or increased levels of activity.

Running Wolf suddenly signaled to stop. His face betrayed his findings.

"Many Mohawk tracks go to village. Not good!" These tracks confirmed our worries and increased our uneasiness. I decided that we needed to discuss how to approach the village without raising suspicion. Observing signs that Mohawk warriors had arrived, probably armed with muskets, so close to our trading area was most worrisome.

"I think it best that I should enter the village alone and talk to the Pocumtucs," I whispered to Running Wolf. "They know me well, and the wampum peace belt of Uncas could be put to good use." I would seem less a threat to any Mohawks in the village than an armed Mohegan. Running Wolf halfheartedly agreed, for he saw this plan as dangerous for both of us. It was a risk to split up, but we knew we needed to discover the intent of these Mohawks and protect our families.

"Wait here, but be ready if I need you," I ordered Running Wolf. He nodded in agreement.

I cautiously began my entrance to the village with my musket slung over my shoulder. I saw no concern as to my presence from the first villagers I encountered, for they knew me from the trading post. As I approached the wetus of the village sachem, I was stopped by a rapidly growing cluster of warriors. I raised my right hand, palm outward, as a sign of peace. The village sachem pushed through the group of warriors.

"Big Knife, you welcome here, but why you come?"

"I come to see the numbers of your furs for trade," I explained. "We need to know so we can tell Pynchon downriver."

"We no more furs for you."

I knew he was lying but had no way of forcing him to tell the truth or explain his lie further. It was then I noticed the well-armed group of warriors nervously standing just to one side of the Pocumtucs. I could tell that these were not Pocumtuc warriors by their dress and mannerisms.

"You got new friends?"

The sachem nodded. "They brother warriors from village to west." It was not a direct lie but not the truth either.

I nodded. "Tell them to bring their furs to trading post."

The sachem stared impassively at me. I now knew that the Mohawks were, in fact, here—and in some numbers. There was no need to continue this conversation with the sachem any further. I thanked the sachem and turned to leave, noticing that the Mohawk warriors were starting to follow me. I turned back to the sachem and offered him wampum beads as a token of friendship. He accepted the wampum beads and offhandedly motioned for the Mohawk warriors to stop. I began thinking about what would have happened if I had not handed over the wampum beads to the sachem. I feared there might still be trouble yet.

I hurriedly rejoined Running Wolf outside the village. We hastily began to retrace our footsteps to our hidden canoe. Suddenly, a musket blast rang out in the forest, and the ball whizzed past our heads! It was a warning shot and was not to be lightly taken. We spotted the puff of musket smoke but not the shooter. A loud war hoop echoed through the trees.

Then we heard another musket blast—this ball flew too close. Running Wolf and I gestured to split up and meet back at the canoe, increasing our chances for safety while decreasing the effectiveness of our

Mohawk pursuers. As we faced each other, we both grinned, knowing that these Mohawk warriors were unfamiliar with these forests.

Running Wolf took off running into the deeper underbrush, while I struck out at a similar pace along a ridgeline paralleling the river. I desperately searched for a rocky outcrop I had noticed on our journeys along this part of the river, thinking that I could use it as a good defensive position. With a little luck, I might reach the outcrop in time. I heard the cracking branches of pursuit behind me.

As I crested a small rise at full run, I spotted the outcrop to my left in a small clearing. *Not a great amount of cover, but it might be enough to shelter me.* I ducked behind the outcrop and primed my musket, knowing full well that pursuit was closing. Two Mohawk warriors cautiously broke the clearing. I knew that they would not have been able to load their muskets on the run, so I had a few moments of advantage. I cocked, aimed, and fired my musket, hitting the lead warrior in the chest. With a grunt, he staggered forward and fell onto his face. He did not move again.

The second warrior turned and ran for the cover of the trees. I hoped that I would not see him again, but to be safe, I waited, holding my breath. Nothing—I heard and saw no movement and no other musket shots, so I guessed that the second warrior had returned to the safety of the village. No other musket blasts echoed through the forests, meaning that Running Wolf was also safe.

After nervously waiting for any further signs of movement, I finally ventured forth from the protective outcrop and slowly walked toward the sprawled Mohawk warrior. I stooped to pick up his musket, noticing it was of Dutch origin, and stowed his shot and powder in my pouches. *This action was in self-defense, for I know that the Mohawk warriors would have killed and scalped me without hesitation. True, I killed O'Malley and Pynchon's workers in fits of vengeful rage. I fired my musket at the Missituc fort, but my shots were not aimed directly at another man. I have never shot and killed a man before! Why are my thoughts wandering like this when my life is threatened so?*

I slipped my machete out of my belt and made ready to hack off the warrior's scalp lock. *Why am I hesitating? This Native tried to kill me!* I could not bring myself to scalp this warrior. It was enough for me to have shot and killed him. *It is a sickening feeling to have taken another's life this way. My intent was to send a warning to the Pocumtucs and their brother Mohawk warriors that if they want war with me, then war they will get. This killing was a justified warning.*

Suddenly, a bloodcurdling war cry escaped my lips. I knew not where this came from. It startled me with its savagery, but it cleared my mind of these wandering thoughts and brought me back to task. I tucked my machete back into my belt, shouldered both muskets, and moved toward the canoe rendezvous with Running Wolf.

* * *

As I approached the brush where the canoe was hidden, Running Wolf stepped out from behind some nearby underbrush. He had been able to evade the Mohawks pursuing him without further conflict. He studied me, noticed the Dutch musket, and then grunted acknowledgment.

"One less Mohawk is good!"

"I'd no choice. They had me cornered. I shot and killed one. The other ran off. I hope the killing warns them off, but it might give them a reason to come back."

If they did come back, I knew their force of numbers could overwhelm us even at the blockhouse with our ammunition supplies. I would need to consider our options once we got back to the trading post. We uncovered the canoe and paddled our way downriver in silence. I sensed that Running Wolf was more than eager to return. It would be good to get back to our families and our safe haven.

As we rounded a big bend in the river, we saw a column of thick black smoke rising above the treetops. Our hearts sank. We knew that the location of the smoke was the trading-post blockhouse. Not knowing the situation there, I decided our best approach was through the forest, with as much cover as possible. We nosed our canoe ashore, jumped out with our muskets, and ran pell-mell through the forest as quietly as possible.

The scene at the trading post was pure chaos. The trading-post blockhouse was in flames. Our possessions, or what remained of them, were strewn about the clearing. Our inventories of pelts and barter goods had been ransacked, and the pelts were gone! At the edge of the clearing, I found Cornsilk leaning against a tree. As I ran to her, I saw that she was naked, and her body was spattered with caked-on blood. It was obvious she had been in a struggle for her life and had lost.

Time seemed to stand still. Her eyes locked onto mine for a brief moment as I kneeled before her, afraid to touch her, not knowing where she was injured or whose blood was covering her. Her lips curled into a smile, as they did every time I came home, and then the spirit inside her drained out. *Is the love of my life dead?* I tenderly wrapped my arms around her, attempting to cover her nakedness with whatever I could find. *Is there any sign of life left in her—a heartbeat, a breath, another last look?*

"Who? ... Why?" I screamed and sobbed and tore at my clothes, but there was nothing I could do to bring her back to life. No amount of shaking would wake her. *She is dead—she is lifeless!* Running Wolf frantically searched for Winged Heart and Smiling Sun without luck. *They are gone! What about my son, Aaron? Where is he? Gone too? Who has taken them? Or are they all dead somewhere out in the forest? Did the raiders take them? We have to know!*

I wrapped Cornsilk in the remnants of our wedding blanket, which I found lying in the grass, closed her eyes, and laid her body at the edge of the clearing. I would tend to her burial later. I needed to find the living first—if they were still alive. Running Wolf confirmed my suspicions that the raiders were white men, probably Puritan colonists from downriver, based on the numerous footprints he discovered in the clearing. This could not have been Pynchon's doing. I would have staked my life on that fact. It had to have been rabble from the colonists downriver or friends of the workers we killed out for revenge.

We attempted to put out the fires, but the damage was done—I had lost everything. *My wife! My son! My trading post and my barter business! All gone! I lost my thin place, my place of peace and happiness.* Running Wolf came to me stone-faced.

"We need find Winged Heart, Smiling Sun, and Aaron. We find now, Big Knife!"

I could not argue. *I need to move on. Yes, we need to find them. We need to go now.* I motioned my readiness to Running Wolf with a slight nod as tears streamed down my face. With one last look over my shoulder to my wife's now-peaceful face, I followed Running Wolf into the forest.

* * *

We searched in vain for any signs or tracks left by our three loved ones in the forests surrounding our trading post. Running Wolf was both a hunter and a tracker. If they were out here somewhere, if they had left any track at all, he would find them. For the rest of that afternoon, we searched without finding a trace. With night coming on, we knew we had to suspend our search. Once all traces of light were gone, we sat opposite each other with our backs against tree trunks, waiting in silence. The only sounds were the hoots of a night owl and our sobs. We both stared into the darkness, trying not to think, overwhelmed by the tragedies, and trying to be patient for the first signs of light.

As morning's light first tipped the treetops, we stood to start anew. After a few steps, suddenly, Running Wolf stopped as if frozen. He bent over and gently moved some leaves. I saw nothing. Running Wolf pointed at a patch of ground.

"It's Winged Heart. She carry heavy load. Look, Smiling Sun." But there were only two sets of tracks. *Where is Aaron?* Running Wolf was now smiling, for he had found his proof of life.

I followed closely behind Running Wolf as he raced in the direction of the tracks. At the edge of a swampy area, Running Wolf again quickly stopped. He had cautioned me to not yell out their names, for they would not respond and it might force them deeper into cover. He whistled a note that sounded like the call of a local songbird. Close by, we heard a responding call. Then, from around a tree, out stepped Winged Heart, holding Aaron in her arms, and Smiling Sun. We rushed to them and embraced them with true joy. They were whole and safe! We would take them back to the site of our trading post and attempt to learn the truth about this raid.

Through much sobbing, Winged Heart began to explain. Running Wolf translated for her.

"Two boats of white men come downriver. We had no fear of them. We wait to unload boats. Supplies? No! They come for us! They carry muskets and pikes. We lost our fight! Cornsilk say to run to the woods! Take Aaron and Smiling Sun. This I did. We watch from forest as they grab Cornsilk, beat, tear off clothes, and ... and then lay on her over and over again! No watch no more. They open blockhouse, take furs and goods. Set fire to it. White men come search for us. We run fast and far to swamp. They could not find us. We knew only Running Wolf could find us."

I had hoped that fully knowing what had happened during the raid would ease my grief, but during her telling, I completely felt the loss. Again I felt my body shake with rage and revenge, but I knew there was no way of discovering who had committed these crimes or where they were now. A search for them would bear no fruit.

* * *

Back at the remnants of our trading post, I went to the body of Cornsilk and began the cleansing rituals for burial. I wrapped her stiff, lifeless body in our bloodied wedding blanket and buried her next to the gravesite of Wolf's Tail. I spent the day by the side of her grave, grieving for both the times we had shared, now only memories, and the future times we would not share.

A good part of my life is now over, my future gone. There is no room for revenge. I was at a loss as to what to do next. *I do have our dearest son, but what kind of future can I give to him? I have now so much less to give him than my father gave to me.* I needed to think hard and make a good decision, but it was difficult to complete thoughts through the waves of rage and grief. *If the Mohawks are on their way to the post, we have little with which to defend ourselves.*

Running Wolf and Winged Heart moved toward me with downcast faces and sad hearts to discuss our futures. True friends, they offered much compassion. They had lost a son and now a sister from this tragedy.

"We must go now," explained Running Wolf, "before Mohawks come."

"I cannot leave yet! I will not leave her!" I knew in my heart that we had to leave, but the tragedy still filled me.

"For safety of Winged Heart and Smiling Sun, we must return to our Mohegan homes, to safety of our people and our village. My family needs our village now. Aaron needs this village too!"

"Yes, of course, I understand, but Aaron must remain with me."

"I give you this for your son, Aaron." With a swift gesture, he produced his ancestral ax.

With trembling hands, I accepted his gift, which I knew had been meant for his son, Wolf's Tail. "You and Aaron come with us?"

"I cannot. I will send Aaron with you. That is for the best for him. If I am seen with you by the settlers downriver, they will ring the alarms and put you and your family in even more danger. You can more easily slip by them without me. I can lead the Mohawks safely away from your trail. They will be searching for a white man. Go now! We will meet again! And, here, take back the ax you gave me for Aaron. It should rightfully go with him."

We hugged as brothers. He turned and slowly moved toward our one remaining canoe. I called him back and handed him the shot, powder, and Dutch musket I had taken from the dead Mohawk warrior. They had nothing more to take with them—just the buckskins on their backs. He and his family did not look back. I briefly held Aaron, clutching him to me as if for the last time.

"Aaron, my son, we must part now, but I will come for you when the time is right. May Manitou, our Great Protector, keep you safe."

Aaron seemed to understand, for he quickly headed for the canoe and tumbled in. I watched them as they slowly paddled downriver. Aaron kept his gaze on me the entire time until they paddled out of sight. I hoped for a safe journey for them to our village.

I realized that with the departure of Running Wolf, his family, and Aaron, I needed to focus on my own plans. *Aaron is safe now with Running Wolf as long as I can move quietly and quickly into the forests and draw the Mohawks to me. I could not travel with Running Wolf and risk his family further. I cannot travel downriver into Agawam, south into the arms of the avenging and angry Puritan colonists. I definitely cannot travel west into Mohawk country. To the north, perhaps there is safety in nothingness, but not for long. Eastward lie the safety of colonists and farms and my brother, Jacob. If I can reach the Mohawk trail a short distance northeast of here, I might reach safety. Yes, I can journey to Bare Cove and reunite with Jacob! But for how long, and will I be welcome there? Is Jacob even alive? I have no way of knowing, for I have heard nothing from him! What will he think of his half-crazed brother?*

It would be a tough and dangerous trek over some mountains and on trails that might be watched, but I told myself it was worth the risk. As I saw it, I really had no other choice.

CHAPTER 15

I thought about my next steps for a journey that must be quick paced yet secretive. That meant I could not pack much and must live off the forests as I journeyed. Some pemmican, dried berries, and wild rice were all the food that I managed to scavenge, along with a small flask for water, one musket, shot, powder, my machete, and a stout bow and a small quiver of arrows. For clothes, I would have to deal with what I wore, the clothes on my back.

Hurry! I must hurry, but I need one last item. I stopped at Cornsilk's grave, mumbled words of love and good bye, stooped, and picked up a small amount of soil from the grave. I placed the dirt in my small ivory container I always carried. I lifted my pack full of supplies onto my back and hastily moved into the forest. I did not have time to inventory or retrieve anything more. *Again I turn my back on my past to move on toward an unknown future.*

I reached a small trail that Running Wolf and I had discovered some time ago; it led north a short distance and then headed northeast toward the Mohawk trail and, finally, eastward toward Boston. The going on this trail could be rough and tiring, for it was not used often; it was more of a simple Pocumtuc hunting trail. I hoped this was a good thing, for the Mohawk warriors might not think to look here. I attempted to hide my progress on this trail, as Running Wolf had taught me, for I could not be overtaken. A good sixty to eighty furlongs by nightfall could give me a good head start and a sense of safety. I could not risk a fire that night to cook food or to warm myself. Hopefully, the weather would remain clear and free of rain or, worse yet, snow.

I staggered up to the top of a small peak and looked back west. I could not see or hear any pursuers, but that did not mean they were not there. As the falling sun threw lengthening shadows, I found a small hummock surrounded by pines, which offered me some protection and dry bedding. It would have to do, for I was exhausted. I thought about Cornsilk, Running Wolf, his family, and Aaron and their unknown progress. Aaron had lost his mother, members of his extended family, and the only home he had ever known. He was a good boy, and I dearly loved him, but I was deeply worried for his safety. He had neither said a word about his mother nor shed a tear. My last thoughts were of him as I curled up and fell instantly to sleep, finally giving in to exhaustion.

*   *   *

It rained that first night, so I woke up stiff and miserable. After a quick meal of pemmican and berries, I pushed onward. After several hours and a few more furlongs, I detected a rustle of movement ahead, so I stopped to safely investigate. *Mohawks or game of some sort?* Just over a small rise, I spied a doe peacefully grazing.

I set my pack and musket down and picked up the bow and arrows. I was not a bad archer, and the bow and arrows would not signal my location to the Mohawks, as would the musket shot. Stealthily I inched toward the doe, notching the arrow as I moved ahead. Luckily, the doe had not caught my movement or my scent. I had a shot at her, but not a great one. I loosed the arrow and watched as it pierced the doe behind the right shoulder. She thrashed and stumbled down. I rushed in with my machete drawn and finished her off. I now had fresh meat, but, unfortunately, most of it would be wasted. I peeled off the hide and rolled it up to use as ground cover at night. *Do I dare risk a fire to roast what I have?* I needed the energy the meat offered, so I had to risk it.

The small fire, amazingly smokeless given the night's dampness, offered heat to dry me off and a source for roasting the deer meat. I felt the better for it. I buried the remains of the deer. Wolves and bears would find it—hopefully, any pursuers would not.

Again my thoughts returned to my son. He amazed me with his steadfastness and awareness. We had done a good job raising him. Then it struck me: *There will be no further "we" in raising him; my life partner is gone!* With much sadness and without further comment, I pushed onto the hunting trail again.

* * *

At the end of the fourth day, I finally stepped onto the main trail, leaving the higher mountains behind me. The bright sunlight warmed me. There were still no signs of pursuit. If the Mohawks had been searching, they would have overtaken me by now. This well-worn trail, used by the Natives for generations to link the western and eastern peoples, would send me on to Boston over easier, rolling-hill terrain with small ponds and streams for water. I decided to spend the night off the trail. I breathed with less anxiety—but no less sorrow—now that I had reached the main trail without incident. The weather cleared, making travel easier on the trail leading me eastward. That night, I rested more peacefully and with a lighter heart.

At daybreak on the fifth day, I found the travel much more to my liking. The morning weather cleared, and the sky was filled with bright sunshine and large, floating white clouds. The trail itself opened wider; it appeared this area saw much more activity. I found it interesting that I had not met anyone traveling this trail; I had seen no one coming up behind me heading east or fronting me headed west. No sooner had this thought crossed my mind than I caught sight of a fellow traveler heading westward toward me—a colonist, ruggedly dressed for the frontier and not as a farmer. I hailed him.

"Friend, where you be headed?"

"No friend you be, heathen!"

I was not expecting his reaction. He pointed his musket menacingly toward me and pulled open the pan. I had forgotten that I looked like a Native, for my hair was long and tied at the back of my head with a hide thong. My beard showed a full week's growth, and my face had been darkly tanned by outdoor life. I was dressed as a Native, with hide leggings, breechclout, vest, and moccasins.

"I am English like you. I mean no harm, but journey to my family plot near Boston."

"So say you. You may be what you say, but you could pass well for a heathen!"

"I ask again, good man, where headed?"

"I head to a trading post a few days west of here, hoping to find work there. A man named Pynchon said I could find work there maybe. Do you know of it?"

"Aye, I do. It was my post, but no more. It's gone—burned and destroyed beyond all hope. It's a good five days' journey from here along the east side of the river. Go further downriver a few days' journey to Agawam to find work there. Pynchon has much work and land. How did you happen to meet up with Pynchon?"

"Actually, ran into his son John Pynchon. Said his father wrote a book, he did, that may set him guilty for heresy. If so, they'll ban and burn it on the commons. I met this John, son of William, just afore yesterday. He talked to me of the success of his father's fur business and your post."

"If all you say be true, then this John Pynchon may be found still in Boston? I needs be to talk with him."

"By now, he be long gone back to Agawam, and William back to England. Taking over his father's business this son John, truth be told."

What a strange turn of events! A man who preached to us of salvation and obedience to God now in risk of heresy! Now gone from this area and probably to London! I was sure he had taken most of his riches with him. I needed to talk with this son about the raid on the trading post.

"Then how far be it to Boston, good man?"

"You be three to four days out of Concord from here, Boston another day. But you best cut your hair and find some English clothes for you. You'll not find others as hesitant to shoot first."

"Thank you, friend. Here's some advice to you as well. Armed and unfriendly Mohawk warriors lie ahead of you. Keep your powder dry and musket well primed so to keep your hair."

"Good advice, and well met," he said in parting, and with a wave of his hand, he proceeded on his journey westward.

I stood there for a moment, and a wry smile creased my face as I thought on the strange twists and turns that my life had taken. I looked forward to discovering exactly what the future held.

I met no other travelers as I pressed onward that day. I had come a goodly distance without incident, and that was good. My fears of pursuit from the west seemed now like bad dreams. My thoughts centered on reunion with Jacob and his wife, Mercy. *By now they must have added to their family, and hopefully the farm has prospered. Fair hope in that for sure.* With my meager food supplies running low, I needed to find farms and colonists willing to feed and shelter me. It would mean begging, but I was past being too proud, for I needed first to survive; the cold and snow of winter would soon be arriving. So onward I treaded.

The countryside I passed through seemed peaceful and quiet. I passed one or two small farm plots but did not approach them, for they appeared too meager to share any surplus. I needed to seek some food and shelter shortly, for my supplies had finally given out at the end of the eighth day of journey. Winter snow clouds scudded across the horizon.

On the afternoon of the ninth day of my march, I entered the small colony village of Concord. This small hamlet sheltered two dozen families, all housed on small communal plots, along with a working mill and meetinghouse. Entering the village, I was struck by the fairness found here. Again I noticed the strange looks and stares from the villagers. I approached one small cabin at the outskirts of the village and asked directions and sought food and shelter from the good woman of the house

"Good day to you, good woman. Could I trouble you for some food and shelter? It's days since I last ate!"

"Aye, I have some corn bread and honey I can share. 'Tis a little strange that a heathen be needing help, though."

"I am an Englishman like you, from Northamptonshire. I seek to reach my brother's plot in Bare Cove, just to the south of here."

"May the Lord save us! You look more like a heathen than the heathens. Where you be coming from then, son?"

"My fur-trading post a week's journey or more west of here, place called Nonotuck on the river. I had to leave to save myself. Thanks be, I have made it safely this far." I sat down on her stoop and gulped down the good bread and honey she offered me.

"Good woman, may I ask the best track to Boston?"

"Take the Trapelo Road east of the village. Follow it right into Boston."

"One more question, good woman. Can I shelter in your barn for the night?"

"You can, but be gone by sunup."

I trudged to the barn, dug into a small mound of hay, and enjoyed the warmth it offered. Once settled, my eyes quickly closed, and snores filled the barn.

* * *

I bypassed Boston and its busy streets and nosy colonists for the safety and security of the surrounding farmlands. I had decided that I would not hazard the journey into Boston by attempting to search for John Pynchon at this time. I could run that search at a later time and not put myself in needless jeopardy. I arrived in Bare Cove exactly at sunset the next day. The trip was now surely ended, but I feared that the journey I faced might be never ending. I knocked on the door of Jacob's now-substantial home and was greeted by a young woman I did not recognize. She screamed in fear at the sight of me—a tired and ragged-looking heathen.

"Good woman, I look for Jacob Smythe! I am his brother, Jonathan!"

Her screams brought the males of the family running for her protection. A sturdy young man pushed the young woman aside.

"There be no Smythes here, you heathen! Get you gone afore I split open your heathen head with this ax!"

"The name is Smythe—Jonathan Smythe! I look for Jacob Smythe, my brother."

"There are no Smythes here! Have not been for five years or more! We moved here then and took over this farm from Goodman Decker! Be gone! Go see him, you idiot heathen!" With that, the young man slammed the door shut.

Could Jacob and his family have died? Moved on? Of course I knew where the Decker farm was located, and I hurried there without hesitation. There were still candles burning in the windows when I arrived, so I hurried to the door. An older woman answered the knocking.

"Goody Decker," I said, for I did recognize her now, "it is I, Jonathan Smythe, looking for my brother, Jacob. Please tell me where I may find him."

"Oh, my Jonathan, you did give me a fright! Let me get Thomas for you!" A more portly version of the Goodman Decker I remembered ambled into view.

"What have we here? Did I hear someone say Jonathan Smythe? And who is this heathen?"

"Yes, it is I, Jonathan Smythe. I come to find my brother, Jacob."

"So the prodigal son returns," said Decker with a chuckle, "and like a heathen no less!"

Somehow I could not see the humor in any of this, but I pretended not to notice.

"I was running a trading post near Agawam in Nonotuck, when we were attacked, my wife killed, and our post destroyed. I have traveled many days to get here. Can you provide me shelter?"

"By the Almighty, we thought you long dead. Jacob heard you were captured by heathens and given up for dead. Come, let us sit by the fire. Refresh yourself, and tell us of your travels, and I will relay to you about your brother. Good woman, clean and feed him first." He ushered me near to the crackling fire, put a plate of vittles in my hands, and begged me to sit. For the next several hours, I retold my story to him—my "capture" by Mohegans and my return to Saybrook Fort. He was aghast at some of the details, especially my relationship with the Natives, but continued to press for more information. When he had finally let me finish, he told me of Jacob.

"About five years ago, your brother, Jacob, received a letter from the governor of this colony, requesting your presence in Boston. Your brother went in your stead. He reported as requested and was notified that the governor's office had received official documents from Barbados. The documents contained a notice of the death of your uncle and a will of testament from your uncle Richard Smythe in which you were named as executor of his estate, inheriting all of his plantation and holdings. Second named was your brother, Jacob. Seems to us that the oldest brother should be first named, but since we all thought you were dead, Jacob was rightfully named executor and inheritor of the estate. Since the plantation and holdings were rich indeed, Jacob and our daughter Mercy and his growing family left for Barbados to claim their rightful holdings. There was no good reason for Jacob and his family to stay here as farmers when they could live as rich plantation owners in Barbados. Last word we have is that all arrived safely and found that plantation and manor house more than satisfactory."

"I know the manor house there well, since I had a goodly hand in building it," I replied. "I am sure that they will find the house and life there more than comfortable. If I had known about the will and had been present here, I would have bequeathed it to Jacob. He will do well there."

"You are a good and honest man, Jonathan. I am sure that your brother will be well pleased to hear of your resurrection! God's will be done!"

After a moment's silence, I said, "Perhaps you could find a way, Goodman Decker, to help me on to a place called Hartford. I have a need to speak with the governor there to tell him of some news."

"Aye, I have heard of this place called Hartford, but what of this news, son?"

"My wife and I, along with her brother and his family, ran a trading post in a place called Nonotuck on the Connecticut River, north of Hartford. It was a good and prosperous business. We were attacked by vengeful colonists and burned out, and my wife was killed. I sent my son, Aaron, on to the Mohegan village. I barely escaped with my own life. I came here in search of safety and with hopes of reuniting with Jacob and his family. That reunion is not possible now."

"Why would you wish to return to the place where you suffered so great a loss?"

His query was pointed but well taken. I did not want to tell him that I was considering reuniting with Running Wolf and my son at the Mohegan village. I fumbled for a reply.

"It's as close as I can get to my piece of heaven on earth. My soul and my son's soul fully live there. There'd be no peace for me here in this colony. I'd always be looked upon as different! I'll return there to be at peace," I replied. I realized then that this escape to Bare Cove had been a foolish and rash plan, even if it had been the only open choice. I had been thinking over this plan of reuniting with my son at the Mohegan village for some time, especially during the last two days of travel. I knew these were words of truth.

Shaking his head, Goodman Decker, with a huge sigh, pushed his bulk from his chair. "We will talk more about this come morn." With that, he snuffed out the candle and left the room.

Tired from my journey, I curled up by the fire. I slept soundly, knowing that I was safe for the time being.

* * *

I decided to winter over with the Deckers, enjoying the peace, harmony, and hospitality of their household as long as I did not venture far from the front gate. I dared not travel to the Sunday services, even though Goody Decker was able to dress me in some secondhand but good Puritan clothing. I worked and served Goodman Decker well, helping with the work of his sizable parcel. I felt it was the least I could do for his generosity.

As the snows of winter gave way to the bounty of spring, I could feel the pull of the forests and mountains to the west and my Mohegan family. I had easily taken on the trappings of the Puritan community, but my heart was still in the forests of the Mohegans. I would venture into the shrinking forests in and around Bare Cove and return with a downturned face and laments about the lack of respect for the spirits of forests. I sought the communion with nature that only the Mohegan village could provide me. I broke the news to Goodman Decker during a warm spring day.

"Father Decker," I said, for that was what I now called him, "the time has come for my return to Connecticut and my Mohegan relatives. I much respect and appreciate your kindness to me, but I need to seek the understanding and knowledge with my son's family."

"Jonathan, I look upon you as a son since your brother, Jacob, and his family are so far off. You are a true and honest lad. I—and Goody Decker as well—will miss you greatly. You know your own mind, so I will respect your wishes. Know, son, you are welcome to return here."

Goodman Decker provisioned me well with a horse, a few coins, and supplies for my travel. I heartily thanked him. With his help, I drafted a letter to Brother Jacob, explaining the events of the past several years and my decision to move back to the Connecticut Colony. With that completed and many thanks, I took my leave the following day and began the journey to return to Aaron and my Mohegan family.

This passage took me through Providence to the lands of the Narragansett and Niantic tribes. I marveled about the outward press of colonization in the area. Farms and small villages were quickly replacing virgin forest. Native brothers were being forcibly pushed from their traditional lands, lands they had known for countless generations. I hoped my Mohegan brothers would be better prepared and safer from these encroachments.

I was easily able to sit astride the horse, which eased my travel westward. Again this journey was to take me ten to fifteen days, and I found that my progress was reported ahead of me—each of the sachems seemed to know of my whereabouts and progress before I reached them. The wampum belt from Uncas was a boon to my travel until I reached the Connecticut Colony.

The Narragansetts were particularly hostile to me, affording me little or no shelter. A brief war in 1643 between the Narragansetts and the Mohegans had ended with the death of the sachem of the Narragansetts, Miantonomo; he was captured and then killed by the Mohegan brother of Uncas, Wawequa. My wampum belt did little to calm their angers, since I was looked upon as part of the family of Uncas and the Mohegans responsible for the death of their sachem. This hostility toward me from my Native brothers was unfamiliar to me, forcing me to move from their lands as quickly as possible. *So the bloody strife continues in this colony—Puritan man against Native man, and Native man against Native man.*

Here in the southern region of the Connecticut Colony, I followed the same route I had taken with Captain Mason and the militia forces over a decade ago when we had marched to the Pequots' Missituc fort through Niantic lands westward along the coast. It felt a trifle strange to be retracing these footsteps that had ended in bloodshed, but I allowed the enveloping forests to calm me. I could not push the thoughts from my mind about belonging here. *Should I be coming here at all and rejoining Running Wolf?* The Deckers had provided loving care for me, but I needed the freedoms I would find only here with my Mohegan clansmen. I knew Running Wolf did not fault me for the tragedies that had befallen our families, and I trusted that his family cared for Aaron as one of their own. *But do I belong here or anywhere near here?*

* * *

After fifteen days of journey, I finally reached Running Wolf's village. I received a joyous greeting. I found Aaron happily playing with children in the village. When he saw me, he ran to me, jumped into my arms, and wrapped his little arms around my neck. Running Wolf came to me and greeted me with smiles and brotherly hugs. Winged Heart took me by the hand and reintroduced me to the rest of the village. They easily received me as a member of the village family. This was a good and warm welcome, and my heart seemed at peace for the first time since leaving Bare Cove over a fortnight ago.

We feasted and smoked the sacred tobacco to honor my return to my brothers and the village. That night, I slept in the family wetus that I had shared with Cornsilk, but sleep did not come easily, for I was filled with loneliness and longing for her. Her spirit overwhelmed me.

The next morning, I awoke to Running Wolf shaking my arm. He motioned for me to step outside the wetus. There, I found Winged Heart, Smiling Sun, and Aaron standing before me.

"Big Knife," said Running Wolf, "we glad you return to us and ask to stay with us."

"Yes, my heart longs to be here. I had hoped that my journey to my brother in Boston would keep the Mohawks from following you. I think that part of my plan worked well. I found that Jacob had long ago journeyed to another land and was not to be found. Foolishly, I'd hoped I could start anew in the Bay Colony and Bar Cove, but my heart was always here. I see now that the right choice is to make my home here with you." I could not tell Running Wolf of the loneliness that filled my heart.

"You know much about our ways; you brother to us. We welcome you. But you not stay here long. You bring white man's anger down on us. They will come for you and destroy us and our ways. To keep us safe, you must leave."

I was shocked to hear this from Running Wolf. I had not thought that by coming here I would place his Mohegan village in danger, but he was right! The colonists from Hartford and Agawam could easily discover that a white man was living in this Mohegan village. The explanations would be difficult, and conclusions might be reached about my reasons for being here. I would be connected to the killings at Pynchon's warehouse. The settlers from Agawam had meted out their form of vengeful justice for crimes against their own. No one in the village would be safe with me here. I would need to harden my heart and leave soon. It was again time for me to journey on, even though I was unsure how much loss Aaron's little heart could take.

The following morning, I was resupplied by Running Wolf and the village and found myself ready to leave the village to face my future on my own. Most of the village gathered to see me off. Aaron tearfully took my hand and led me to the edge of the village.

"Father, I love you, and when I become a man, I'll come to you."

"Running Wolf will teach you well in your passage to becoming a man. You are already well on your way, and I am proud of you. I will look every day for your coming, and that day will be soon." I knelt down, and we embraced as father and son.

"I promise I will send word of my whereabouts to you and to Running Wolf." My thoughts returned to his namesake, his mother, and the passages that had led to this time. I quietly whispered to Aaron, "Off I go, and may Manitou, our Great Spirit, keep you safe."

* * *

My heavy footsteps carried me along the river without heed of direction. My thoughts followed my footsteps, aimlessly wandering. I was in a daze, unfeeling and unmoved by my surroundings. If I walked through water, I was unaware. If I was bitten by insects, I did not feel it. I slept at night huddled in my clothes, stopping only because I could not blindly venture farther in the darkness. I awoke each morning and trudged on, ever away from the Puritan colonies, farther from my Mohegan family. I was a pitiful sight—a man of dirty rags and vacant eyes, seeking out no one for comfort or kind words. I lived on berries and meager game that I could easily seek.

A summer morning found me standing in a spot along the riverbank that looked uncommonly familiar to me. I reacted with a violent start when I realized that I was standing before the graves of my beloved wife, Cornsilk, and our nephew, Wolf's Tail. Without realizing my whereabouts or direction, I had traveled back to where I had started months before. *I have come full circle.*

The charred and barren remains of my former life were a stark reality that fully awakened me. I was heartened to have returned here, but I could not remain here in this site of past happiness and now overwhelming sadness. This was a passage in my life that was now over and completed—a chapter that was fully ended. I had needed to return here one last time to clear my conscience. I had returned, and now I must leave. Sadly, I turned and left, vowing never to return alive.

I continued my trek northward along the river, searching for the large Pocumtuc settlement I knew was north of here—a village that they had named Deerfield in their language. This village sat at the meeting of the Connecticut and a smaller river and was close to the Mohawk trail to the north. At last reaching the village, I was graciously welcomed by the village sachem, whom I knew from past dealings at my trading post. He seemed to know of the tragedies that had befallen me.

"Big Knife, you faced death here in your life journey, yet you return."

"I have nowhere else to go, Sachem. Yes, I faced death in my journey, but my path, right or wrong, led me back here." *As suddenly as my thin place was revealed to me years past, I now see that my death holds no mastery over me in my journey. There is no fear of death, no longing for it.*

"You need to seek your spirit in our mountains and forests, my brother. Come, counsel with our wise man; he will set you on the right path."

I meekly accepted his offer, for I had no other.

The sachem ushered me to the wetus of the wise man. He was an old man who must have been the brother of the woman who had cured M'Gey some years past. Wrinkled with age and toothless, he beckoned me with a thin, clawlike finger to sit before him. I did as I was told. I noticed the intense vapors and pungent fumes rising from a small fire in front of him. He chanted in his language and waved a fan of feathers, moving the vapors and fumes toward me. I coughed and choked but remained steadfast, wishing to learn from this man. I felt my eyelids slowly closing. I was tired and felt defeated; these were the last things I remembered.

I awoke two days later in another wetus with a clear head and a clearer purpose. I was completely and fully rested and was famished and thirsty. As if knowing my feelings, a village woman brought me pemmican and succotash to eat and fresh springwater to drink. Then the wise man and sachem came to me.

"Big Knife, your spirit is born again. You go now on your right path?" The sachem and wise man stared at me, waiting for an answer.

"Yes, Sachem, my path leads me to the mountains north of here. There I can find my peace and begin my life anew." *These words—where did they come from? I had no plan to follow when I first came here! Now I do!*

The wise man smiled knowingly at me, nodding in agreement.

Yes, I will follow this plan and find peace for myself in the solitude of these mountain forests. I asked that the sachem send a messenger to the Mohegan village at Shantok to tell them of my basic whereabouts.

The next day, after thanking the sachem and the wise man, I left this Pocumtuc village, with a lighter heart and mind, in search of my future cabin site. I would need food supplies, an ax, a saw, and some nails—these I could barter for with the Pocumtucs here. This was not the life passage I had thought I would take, but at least I now had a plan for a peaceful life, a life of solitude, a life of thankfulness. And then there were Aaron and Running Wolf and the hope of reuniting with them in a short span of time. *Yes, here too there is hope!*

Epilogue

But let every man prove his own work,
and then shall he have rejoicing in himself alone,
and not in another.
For every man shall bear his own burden.
Galatians 6:4–5

Far North of Deerfield—Autumn 1665

My face was now deeply creased by time and weathered from the seasons and the mountain wilderness; my white hair was full and long, tied at the back of my neck with a thin length of rawhide in the manner of the Mohegans. My buckskin clothing smelled of sweat, gunpowder, and slight tinges of aged brandy, but I focused my thoughts on my hands and thick, calloused fingers as telltale signs of the passages I had endured.

My hand-hewn log cabin lay deep in the wilderness land north of Nonotuck, on a large, rocky mountain outcrop that hid the storage cave behind it. It was a place of safety. The village of the Pocumtucs where I had found my new life passage lay not far off, but far enough off. This peaceful place was as far into the mountains and forests as I dared to venture. The forested land was bountiful here and free from most troubles. It was also to my favor that few colonists were here so far to the north, but I discovered that the local Pocumtucs with whom I frequently traded suffered much from the pox brought by the settlers and traders and their ongoing skirmishes with the raiding Mohawks. My Mohegan family still lived near the fort of Uncas, who remained the sachem. I had learned secondhand that my brother, Jacob, and his family in Barbados had mightily prospered, and the Deckers had enlarged their holdings in Bare Cove. My now-distant family's happiness was a source of joy for me, and I wished them well. I harbored no remorse as to my decision not to return there.

Running Wolf had eventually found me in my mountain retreat and returned Aaron to me some five years past, once my son had passed the trials of manhood in our Mohegan village. Running Wolf and the Shantok village there had taught him much. Now in his twentieth autumn, he carried the name of White Wolf as a full Mohegan warrior of the Shantok Wolf clan, as well as his given name of Aaron. Running Wolf and I remained brothers in blood, bonded these many years, our lives entwined with the journeys and passages we traveled together. Now it would be Aaron's turn to honor our spirits.

The old, rickety wooden stool on which I sat was positioned before a small, crackling fire. My son was squatted in front of me on the dirt floor of our tiny cabin. Early fall winds whipped around the outside of the cabin, making the heat from the fire inside warm and welcome. It was good to be with him, my son, in this vast wilderness. I eagerly sought the passing of my own wisdom to him for the start of his journeys to come. It seemed strange to me that I had not until now told him of my own passages. Perhaps it was better to have waited until he was old enough to fully understand. A single tear slowly tumbled from the corner of my eye as I looked at him.

"Son, this was not a telling easy told. Something I've carried with me as a young man newly journeyed to this country. But it's true as I'm sitting here. A part of your family's history so you'll know what I saw, what I did, and why I did it." I paused in my telling as my hand went to my neck, where it caressed a keepsake held there by a rawhide thong.

"As you now know, this was the reason for the start of my journey, these passages, and the choice for your name."

I fully bore the burdens of my decisions and the passages endured. The peacefulness of my life in these mountain forests gave me the time to measure myself against the rhythms of the seasons and to gain an understanding of my rightful place in nature. With my tale to Aaron now ended, I realized that I still was haunted by what I had lost—my beloved wife and my trading post, with little monetary gain to show—but I had reaped a true legacy: my son, Aaron. I was proud of him, the stout-hearted young man I had learned to fully love. It was a gain truly worth receiving.

I told him that I wished to be honored as a Mohegan when my time came, buried farther south along the river next to the graves of Cornsilk, my wife and his mother, and my nephew, Wolf's Tail. It was a sacred spot to us. I handed on to Aaron the wampum belt of Uncas and my coveted machete, and along with Running Wolf's battle ax, he proudly carried them in his journeys through the forests. In his own passage, he carried much more, for he stood with one foot in the white man's world and one foot in the Mohegan world. I saw that he cherished both worlds, for he clearly saw the good in both.

Aaron bore with him one other treasured gift—the ivory tooth carved with my initials, complete with a rawhide thong he wore tied around his neck. The container safely held the spirits of Aaron Carpenter, Wolf's Tail, and Cornsilk. In a day soon to come, when my journey was ended, Aaron knew to set free all of our spirits at our sacred place by the river to mingle the soil of their thin places with that of my own so that we could journey together to join Manitou, our Great Spirit. Our true passages would then have finally reached our peaceful resting places.

Historical Notes and Acknowledgments

England in the seventeenth century was politically and religiously in turmoil. With the death of the childless Queen Elizabeth in 1603, the reign of the Tudors was over. James VI of Scotland, son of Mary, Queen of Scots, a Stuart and Elizabeth's closest Protestant relative, was crowned king of England as James I. Upon taking his coronation in 1603, King James made peace with Spain, thereby giving England a somewhat stable and peaceful period for the duration of his short reign. King James, a devout Protestant, ordered the translation and transformation of the Bible, creating the authorized King James Version that endured for centuries. His reign ended with his death in 1625, but not before the start of English colonization in the New World: Jamestown in Virginia in 1607, Bermuda in 1609, and Plymouth in 1620. English settlers began arriving in England's fourth colony, Barbados, in 1627.

However, trouble truly began with the ascension of Charles I to the throne in 1625. He married a Catholic princess, Henrietta Maria of France; believed totally in divine ordination and royal prerogatives; increased his landholdings and domination in Ireland; and consistently fought with Parliament, fomenting the English Civil War and leading to his beheading in 1649. This was also the period of English history when the lords and barons attempted to take control of their holdings by moving to more pastoral settings, decreasing the amounts of arable lands for their tenants in favor of pasturage for livestock.

Charles Stuart attempted to move the Church of England from Calvin Puritanism to a more traditional and sacramental form of devotion, which increased suspicions among Puritans about his objectives to return to more Catholic traditions. This played no small role in the Great Migration of Puritans, during which more than twenty thousand Puritans immigrated to the Massachusetts Bay Colony from 1625 to 1640. His alliance with the bumbling courtier George Villiers, the first Duke of Buckingham, led to a costly war with Spain and increased taxes and fees, nearly bankrupting the country and causing further distress to the populace. These events set the stage for this memoir of passage.

I have tried, as far as possible, to be honest with the actual history of this period and the notable people who lived then in seventeenth-century England, Barbados, and the colonies of the New World. John and Henry Winthrop; Captains John Mason, John Underhill, and John Endecott; Lieutenant Colonel Lion Gardiner; and William Pynchon are documented and prominent historic figures. Their interactions with the main character of this fiction, Jonathan Smythe, are based on my imagination and never actually occurred. William Pynchon's book *The Meritorious Price of Our Redemption* was printed in 1650 in London and banned and burned in Boston in 1651. I chose to place the banning in 1650 to keep this action close to Jonathan's escape from Nonotuck. I would like to think that I treated all of these figures fairly during the course of my telling.

Most of the places referenced in this fiction did or still do exist, including Badby Village and Wood, Agawam, Nonotuck, Bare Cove, Duxbury, Oxford, Portsmouth, and the Atlantic Ocean islands visited on Jonathan's crossing voyage. There was no Smythe plantation on Barbados as far as my research reveals. As for the Pequot War and the massacres that occurred, I returned time and again to reference the revisionist history of David R. Wagner and Jack Dempsey, *Mystic Fiasco: How the Indians Won The Pequot War* (2010, Digital Scanning Inc.), which "exposes the fundamental but unexamined paradigms that hard-wired the American colonial psyche from those days to these." Their very plausible and revealing research on this war and its effects on the Native tribes of New England made the most sense to me and to my story, as opposed to the well-known historic narratives of Captains Mason and Underhill and the writings of Reverend Mather. The battle at Missituc did historically occur, but the events as portrayed in this novel are imaginary. I also heavily relied on the extensive historical research compiled by Nick Bunker in *Making Haste from Babylon: The Mayflower Pilgrims and Their World: A New History* (2010, Alfred A. Knopf). This new and imaginative look at the Puritans and their reasons for seeking their freedoms and, yes, fortunes in the New World laid solid foundations for my own writing.

Some of the events in this novel were created from my own family's anecdotes and my genealogic research. I can claim credit to a paternal ancestor who journeyed from Badby Village in England to Massachusetts in 1637 and, shortly following his arrival, was "drafted" into the militia to fight the Pequots in Connecticut. Another of my family members traveled from England to his uncle's plantation in Barbados in 1670 and, on a later voyage to the New England colonies, survived the sinking of his ship; afterward, he was joyously reunited with his father in Lyme, Connecticut. In these cases, the realities of life and its truths are far stranger than the frail and imagined possibilities of this humble work of fiction.

* * *

The biblical quotations at the start of each of the parts are taken from an old family Bible printed in 1848—containing the Old and New Testaments, translated out of the original tongues and with the former translations diligently compared and revised.* This Bible also contains quill-penned family records—births, marriages, and deaths of family members, with births dating back to 1799.

I would like to thank my daughter, Meghan, a college mental health counselor in Maryland, for her critical reviews, directions, and proofreading talents in the finalization of this work. And, of course, without the strength, support, and good humor of my loving wife, Sheila Anne, this novel would never have been started or seen to completion.

Howard Root
February 2013

* *The Holy Bible* (New York: American Bible Society, 1848).